Stories
for
Pleasure

Literature for Life Series

STORIES
FOR
PLEASURE

Selected and introduced by Barrie Wade

Nelson

Thomas Nelson and Sons Ltd
Nelson House Mayfield Road
Walton-on-Thames Surrey
KT12 5PL UK

Nelson Blackie
Wester Cleddens Road
Bishopbriggs
Glasgow G64 2NZ UK

Thomas Nelson Australia
102 Dodds Street
South Melbourne
Victoria 3205 Australia

Nelson Canada
1120 Birchmount Road
Scarborough Ontario
M1K 5G4 Canada

First published by Arnold Wheaton 1985
ISBN 0-560-55001-4

This edition published by Thomas Nelson and Sons Ltd 1992

I(T)P Thomas Nelson is an International
Thomson Publishing Company

I(T)P is used under licence

ISBN 0-17-432279-8
NPN 9 8 7 6 5 4

Printed in China

For Ann

CONTENTS

ACKNOWLEDGEMENTS

The editor and publishers wish to thank the following who have kindly given permission for the use of copyright material:

J. M. Dent & Sons Ltd for Bill Naughton's 'The Sad Fate of the Blue Kite' from *My Pal Spadger*

Faber and Faber Ltd for Ted Hughes' 'The Rain Horse' from *Wodwo*

David Higham Associates Ltd for Dorothy Whipple's 'A Friend' from *The Other Day*, published by Michael Joseph, and for Dal Stivens' 'The Pepper-Tree' from *Spar*, published by Angus and Robertson (F. W. Cheshire Pty Ltd, Victoria, Australia, 1959)

Hutchinson Publishing Group Ltd for J. C. Badcock's 'The Tree' from *The Truants* and for Arthur Barton's 'Football Crazy' from *The Penny World*

Macmillan London Ltd for Walter Macken's 'The Lion' from *Winter's Tales* and for 'The Kiss' from *The Coll Doll and Other Stories*, also by Walter Macken

Penguin Books Ltd for Philippa Pearce's 'What the Neighbours Did' from *What the Neighbours Did and Other Stories* (Puffin Books 1975) pp. 7–21 copyright © Philippa Pearce 1959, 1967, 1969, 1972

A. D. Peters & Co. Ltd for Liam O'Flaherty's 'Mother and Son' from *The Short Stories of Liam O'Flaherty*, published by Jonathan Cape Ltd

Laurence Pollinger Ltd and the Estate of Mrs Frieda Lawrence Ravagli for D. H. Lawrence's 'Adolf' from *Phoenix*, published by William Heinemann Ltd

Laurence Pollinger Ltd and the William Saroyan Literary Foundation for William Saroyan's 'The First Day of School' from *Little Children*, published by Faber and Faber Ltd

Note Up to the time of going to press we have been unable to obtain the necessary permission to reproduce Jack Cope's 'Power' from *Tales of South Africa*, published by Howard B. Timmins (Pty) Ltd, Cape Town, South Africa.

INTRODUCTION

STORIES are a powerful resource for learning. By enabling young readers to involve themselves in other people's lives as onlookers they encourage more than an egocentric, child's-eye view of events and human issues. They influence attitudes, beliefs and values; they refine sensibilities; they sharpen critical intelligence; they help people cope with growing up; they offer a particularly rich vein of experience for contemplation; their narrative pattern heightens and encourages the reader's sensibilities and imaginative powers so that present events are made meaningful by prediction and reflection. Above all, stories give pleasure.

The immense satisfaction that young people gain from reading good stories makes those stories the ideal medium for exploring in depth appropriate topics of concern. Stories also educate the emotions (though not separately from the mind) in a way which most media and areas of the school curriculum cannot. This process is an indirect one since, as well as receiving pleasure and delight, the reader can enter into situations that might otherwise be too complex and too subtle for young understanding.

This collection provides thirteen stories which have given pleasure and delight to adolescents in the English classrooms where I have taught. They continue to give satisfaction to me whenever I share or explore them. Both the sharing and the exploration are acts of pleasure for all concerned.

There are indeed these further pleasures to be obtained from reflection and from exploring a story together, from recreating it imaginatively or from using it as a springboard to talk, writing, drama or other reading. In order to encourage these kinds of activities I have provided a number of Starting points after each story. These are not abstract, nor critical/analytical, but they do lead to rereading, reflection and possibilities of further satisfaction. Thus, while the stories can be enjoyed simply for their own sake, they can be quarried for the additional delight that comes from co-operatively exploring their form and meaning.

I owe a particular debt of gratitude to all the people in my classrooms who increased my satisfaction and insight into these stories while developing their own. I am also grateful to Margaret Hier for her help in preparing the manuscript and to many teachers who have given advice and encouragement. One of these, my wife, Ann, made many valuable suggestions about the contents and the Starting points. The collection is dedicated to her.

Barrie Wade

THE SAD FATE
OF THE
BLUE KITE

Bill Naughton

THERE was one strict rule about going to bed on Thursday nights when I was a boy – *Be sure to shut the bedroom window!* And this shutting of the window was especially important if you – as I did – slept in the back bedroom that overlooked the back street. Furthermore, if it chanced to be summertime, and the wind was coming your way, you had better seal the cracks up with old newspaper. Otherwise, unless you were lucky enough to sleep through it all, you might be in for a somewhat unpleasant ordeal.

The reason for such strict precautions was simply that Thursday night was the occasion for the Night Soilsmen making their weekly visit. Now who or what are Night Soilsmen? it might be asked, since the term is one unlikely to be found in a dictionary. I'll tell you. They usually worked in threes on the job of emptying privy closets, which were very common up to the late 1920s. In fact there were no water-closets in those days – not, that is, within a fair distance of our street in Bolton. The accepted name was privy or privy closet, but it was usually referred to as closet or more often petty by local people.

Petties were set in pairs – and still are, where the houses have not been demolished – back to back, each home with its own, one for you and one for your next-door neighbour, down at the bottom of the backyard, abutting on the back street. A not uncommon call at the time – especially in the homes where there were big families and a queue tended to form after mealtimes – which could be heard along the length of low-walled backyards, was someone at the back door calling to the person occupying the seat: 'Hy! – how much longer are you goin' to be? – D' you want me to fetch the oil-can?'

Of course in the better-off districts, a few streets away, they had what were known as *tippler closets*. But the little scene I'd like to tell about had to do with an ordinary privy closet. It happened in the

1

backyard of my mate Spadger. I was in there with him one lovely hot sunny afternoon in July helping him to build a kite. I say build and not make because the kind of kite we were working on you always said build since it was known as a Big Bender. The centre upright piece was as long as Spadger was tall – an inch more in fact – and the cross-piece was like a mighty bow from which you could have shot an enormous arrow. In a way it compared with one of these huge model aeroplanes you get in these days.

We had been working on it from early morning. First we had gone to the cane yard where they made skips for the cotton mills, and we had spent a long time selecting the two splendid canes that cost us a halfpenny each. An absolutely firm one for the upright, and a slightly flexible one for the cross-piece. Then we had gone to a special paper shop in town where we had spent twopence on huge sheets of the most marvellous blue tissue paper, light in weight but strong. The string we got for nothing, from a boy who worked at the ropeworks, where they made it. Next we had spent hours in getting a perfect balance for the cross-piece. You had only to be the least fraction of an ounce out in the balance and your kite would pull to one side, or it might even start ducking. And now we had cadged some flour from my mother, and mixed our paste, and we were just getting going with the pasting down of the paper over the string.

It was all very tricky work, and I could never have managed it without old Spadger, who had very nimble fingers. In fact if anyone had asked us why we were doing it I doubt if we could have answered. I think what brought it about was the warm sunshine. Amongst those dense streets and all that smoke-laden atmosphere it seemed that the sunshine had a hard job getting through, and most days it sort of gave up before breakfast time. But when it did get through it seemed to send folk mad, and they started doing the daftest things. There was a neighbour lived a couple of doors from us who suddenly decided that instead of paying her rent and other things she would take the kids off to Blackpool for a day. You only live once, she said, and they'd never seen the sea. It took her years to get straight. One chap at the top of the street went off to Wigan to see his brother Joe, whom he hadn't seen for twenty years. When he got there Joe was out. Spadger and myself decided to build the best and biggest kite ever seen around those parts. And even though we had spent all our money on that kite, we knew we should have a pretty hard job getting it airborne.

It seemed you never got a breath of wind in those streets, unless it happened to be coming from a peculiar direction. Anyway, once you got your kite up over the housetops you were away, for the masses of chimney pots, which smoked day and night, and also high mill chimneys created a sort of upward pull, and if you got your kite into a thermal current it would rise very rapidly, and before you knew where you were that kite could be almost out of sight.

Anyway, there are Spadger and myself down on our knees in their backyard, feeling a bit drytongued and weary with all the concentration it needed as we applied the paste to stick the paper down. But a most beautiful kite was slowly taking shape. In fact it had taken shape. We were just putting the finishing touches to it. I daren't let myself look at it yet, for it was such a handsome kite it would take your breath away. Then suddenly we heard a scream that set our nerves on edge.

I looked at Spadger. He had this face that looked different from other lads. I don't know how it is, but if you're brought up in a town that is noisy, sort of industrial, with mill buzzers hooting away, folk clattering about in clogs with irons on the bottom, and nearly everybody talking in loud voices, some of them yelling out, it seems to happen that most faces take on two main kinds of looks: they're either grinning or scowling. Not much in between. Spadger had a calm expression. Very rare in those parts. I suppose that is why it always sticks so clearly in my mind. He had what they call a broad forehead, and what with being quick on his feet nobody had ever managed to land him one on his conk, so that his nose was a good clean shape, and his cheekbones were just that bit raised, and he had large quiet eyes.

Whilst making the kite he had come across a square of blue paper that was over and with a few folds and twists he had made it into a sort of carnival hat. 'I don't want to be struck with a very rare complaint,' he said to me. I said: 'What's that?' And he said: 'Sunstroke in Bolton.' And whilst I was thinking his remark over, and looking at him with this peculiar blue hat on his head, there came this scream, fairly close at hand.

We both jumped up on to our feet and darted to the privy closet from where the scream had come. Spadger shoved the door open. There was a wild screech for help. And then we saw what had happened. Cyril, Spadger's young brother, who was five years old, or he might been six, but he was on the short side, must

3

have been playing on the privy closet seat, standing up and messing around – as I say, everybody went a bit daft – and his foot must have slipped, and he had fallen through the hole, and there he was up to his knees in the pail. As bad luck would have it the day of the week was Thursday, so that the pail was full almost to the top. And a further bit of bad luck was that as he tried to lift himself out his hands slipped and fell into the pail. Now he had lost his nerve altogether and was flinging his arms about yelling for someone to lift him out.

Spadger spoke to him soothingly and was about to give a hand and pull him out, but when Cyril stretched his hands out they were covered, so that even old Spadger hesitated. 'Get me out!' yelled Cyril. 'Get me out!'

'Hold on a tick, Cyril,' Spadger called back, 'I'll get the clothes-prop – you'll be able to hold on to that and hoist yourself out.'

Cyril didn't think much of that idea, and whilst Spadger nipped back into the backyard for the long clothes-prop he went on shrieking at the top of his voice as though he were drowning, when in fact there was no actual danger, beyond that of his getting even more messed up than he already was. I might say I kept myself pretty clear. Yet I couldn't take my eyes off him. By this time half the neighbourhood was out, looking over backyard walls, back gates, or squinting through their back bedroom windows. They wanted to know what all the fuss was about. The way it was in those times, there was no television of course, no wireless sets, and very little to fill in one's time, so that a lad down a privy closet was quite a juicy item on a hot afternoon. Not something to be missed.

The next thing Spadger was back with the clothes-prop. He calmed young Cyril down with his calm voice as he wedged one end into the corner wall of the privy, and he and I held the other end, so that Cyril could get hold of the top and sort of lift himself out. It seemed to be a very good idea, as indeed were most of Spadger's ideas, and Cyril grabbed the prop with both hands and muscled himself up with a spring, so that in a trice he was up above the seat. But just then it happened that the end of the clothes-prop that was wedged into the wall must have come against a piece of loose brick or plaster, for the next thing it suddenly slid downwards. Cyril let out a squawk and made a scramble, but he was just a second too late, so that this time he fell

4

with his backside back into the pail. Which as I have said was filled almost to overflowing. In fact it did overflow.

Cyril seemed to be getting into more of a mess, and was clamouring away like mad, so that Spadger put down the prop and called out: 'All right, Cyril – keep calm. And I'll lift you out.' The trouble was, Cyril had somehow got his knees below the hole in the wooden seat of the privy closet, so that when he bent his knees to try to extricate himself they got caught under the hole. Then just as Spadger was approaching to lift Cyril out, the back gate suddenly opened and in came Spadger's and Cyril's Mum. It seems she had been in the corner shop when she heard all the commotion and the news had reached her of something out of place in the closet.

'Stop! – what's up?' she called out.

'Our Cyril's fell into the petty hole,' said Spadger, hesitating. 'He wants lifting out.'

'Then let him fall out again,' said his Mum. 'Don't you go near him – I'll have enough bother gettin' him clean. I don't want two of you messed up.'

'Mum...! Mum...!' shrieked old Cyril. It was pitiful to hear him. 'Lift me out! Lift me out, Mum!'

Cyril had his arms raised in appeal, but they looked a mess they did, for it was all running down his jersey. 'Not likely,' said his Mum. 'Not with you in that state. What do you take me for? You got yourself in so's now you can get yourself out. An' give over flailin' your blinkin' arms about – you're messin' up the walls.' Mothers weren't so soft in those days.

It seems a funny thing in this life, but if people refuse to help you and you find there's nothing for it but helping yourself, you seem to get energy or something from somewhere, and the next thing young Cyril had given one angry squirm and spring and he is up through that privy hole and standing out in the backyard. We retreated pretty sharp. I might say he didn't look too good. He was covered in the stuff. It was dripping off him. There was a bit of a hum too. It was a summer day.

'Mum! Mum!' he wailed, holding his hands out to his mother. 'What'll I do?'

'You keep your distance,' warned his mother.

'See that, Bill,' whispered Spadger to me, as we quickly put our lovely big blue kite into a corner out of the way. We weren't having any harm come to that.

5

'See what?' I said.

'Keep away from my kitchen,' yelled Cyril's Mum as he tried to make his way indoors. 'Don't you dare set foot in there!' Then she grabbed a big yardbrush and drew it back as though it were a golf club or a cricket bat. Any notion Cyril may have had of forcing his way inside seemed to leave him at the sight of his Mum with that long brush, ready to swipe.

'You could fall into a ragin' sea,' said Spadger to me, 'an' like as not some stranger will come along an' risk his life for you. Or you could be up to your throat in quicksand an' somebody would help you out before you got sucked under. But if you fall down a privy closet even your own mother doesn't want to know.'

'Can't say I blame her,' I said.

'Mum! Mum!' squealed Cyril, ' – what'll I do?'

'You shoulda thought of that before you fell in,' said his mother. Then she tugged the short length of hosepipe off the wall, nipped in through the kitchen door, bolting it behind her, and the next thing she had the back kitchen window open and the hosepipe through. She fastened it to the kitchen tap and turned on the water and a jet of water shot out and then she called out: 'Spadger, hose him down.'

Cyril didn't fancy that and he let out further howls. Spadger didn't seem to care for the idea either. 'Won't he catch a cold, Mum?' he said.

'There are worse things than colds,' said his mother. 'Hose him down when I tell you.' Then she called to Cyril: 'An' you start gettin' your things off – or else I'll have you back in that privy pail an' let the muck-misers take you off to Wellington sewage yard tonight. They'll soon get you clean there.' With women like that you can never be sure when they are joking or not, so Cyril stood there ready to be hosed down. 'Keep near the grid,' she shouted. 'I don't want it all over my backyard.'

'Don't crouch up, Cyril,' said Spadger, as he began with the hose on Cyril, 'just stick your chest out. You won't feel it as much.' That was a funny thing about Spadger, he was never one to laugh at you when you were in trouble. There are not many mates you can say that about and even fewer brothers. 'That's it, Cyril,' he went on, 'take it on the chest.'

At first Cyril did not like it. But then who would? Spadger had to have the hose going very hard to get the stuff off. Now I can't say what came over Cyril during the next minute or two, but as he kicked off his clogs and socks, and then his jersey and shirt and everything, with the water shooting full at him, and at last stood naked in that backyard, it seemed as though he suddenly found that he was enjoying himself. Perhaps it was the tonic effect of the cold water, or it may be that it was the first time he had stood in his bare skin with not a stitch on in the open air, or it may have been all the folk that were looking on from all over the place, but whatever it was he started dancing around. For a moment I thought he'd gone off his head with the shock. The next thing he pretended he was a gorilla and let out a whooping growl and began scratching under his armpits and at the same time he began singing: 'I'm crazy about bananas, monkey nuts an' grapes, That's why they call me Tarzan of the Apes!'

And with that he went leaping about that backyard like a great big ape or monkey or something, jumping up on a ladder and then on to a bucket, and all the time yelling for Spadger to give him more water.

'Bill!' called Spadger. 'Watch it – our kite!'

I spotted the danger but I was too late to stop it. I mean not only was Cyril going around like a whirling dervish, but there was still some of the stuff flying off him, so in a way I had to keep my distance. So I prayed – but it didn't seem to make all that difference. He made one of his fantastic spins that took him right into the corner where our kite was safely stacked up. The next thing he gave a wild leap into the air, and landed with his backside right in the middle of the kite. First you could hear the paper bursting as he landed clean on top of it, and after that you could hear the mighty cross-piece crack and split. When I opened my eyes again there was Cyril set right in the middle of our smashed kite, laughing his blooming head off.

Starting points

1. *Talk about a time when you spent a lot of care and effort making something and then somebody else spoiled it. Was it by accident or on purpose? How did you feel? Write an entertaining story to be read by your classmates about your experience.*

2. *Talk about Spadger's Mum, the way she felt, how she acted and what she said. Does she behave like this because these events happened a long time ago? Would a mother who had lots of hot water and a washing-machine act differently? Have you ever been treated unsympathetically by adults?*

3. *Working in pairs, act out a scene in the corner shop when a neighbour who has watched the whole episode comes in and re-tells it to the shopkeeper. One person takes the part of the neighbour, the other plays the shopkeeper.*

4. *(a) Look again at the parts of the story which describe Spadger and talk about what he looks like and what kind of person he is as well as how he behaves in the story.*

   (b) Re-read the part where Cyril acts unusually when he is being hosed down. Why do you think he behaves as he does?

THE
FIRST DAY
OF SCHOOL

William Saroyan

HE was a little boy named Jim, the first and only child of Dr Louis Davy, 717 Mattei Building, and it was his first day at school. His father was French, a small heavy-set man of forty whose boyhood had been full of poverty and unhappiness and ambition. His mother was dead: she died when Jim was born, and the only woman he knew intimately was Amy, the Swedish housekeeper.

It was Amy who dressed him in his Sunday clothes and took him to school. Jim liked Amy, but he didn't like her for taking him to school. He told her so. All the way to school, he told her so.

I don't like you, he said.

I don't like you any more.

I like *you*, the housekeeper said.

Then why are you taking me to school? he said.

He had taken walks with Amy before, once all the way to the Court House Park for the Sunday afternoon band concert, but this walk to school was different.

What for? he said.

Everybody must go to school, the housekeeper said.

Did you go to school? he said.

No, said Amy.

Then why do I have to go? he said.

You will like it, said the housekeeper.

He walked on with her in silence, holding her hand. I don't like you, he said. I don't like you any more.

I like you, said Amy.

Then why are you taking me to school? he said again.

Why?

The housekeeper knew how frightened a little boy could be about going to school.

You will like it, she said. I think you will sing songs and play games.

9

I don't want to, he said.

I will come and get you every afternoon, she said.

I don't like you, he told her again.

She felt very unhappy about the little boy going to school, but she knew that he would have to go.

The school building was very ugly to her and to the boy. She didn't like the way it made her feel, and going up the steps with him she wished he didn't have to go to school. The halls and rooms scared her, and him, and the smell of the place too. And he didn't like Mr Barber, the principal.

Amy despised Mr Barber.

What is the name of your son? Mr Barber said.

This is Dr Louis Davy's son, said Amy. His name is Jim. I am Dr Davy's housekeeper.

James? said Mr Barber.

Not James, said Amy, just Jim.

All right, said Mr Barber. Any middle name?

No, said Amy. He is too small for a middle name. Just Jim Davy.

All right, said Mr Barber. We'll try him out in the first grade. If he doesn't get along all right we'll try him out in kindergarten.

Dr Davy said to start him in the first grade, said Amy. Not kindergarten.

All right, said Mr Barber.

The housekeeper knew how frightened the little boy was, sitting on the chair, and she tried to let him know how much she loved him and how sorry she was about everything. She wanted to say something fine to him about everything, but she couldn't say anything, and she was very proud of the nice way he got down from the chair and stood beside Mr Barber, waiting to go with him to a classroom.

On the way home she was so proud of him she began to cry.

Miss Binney, the teacher of the first grade, was an old lady who was all dried out. The room was full of little boys and girls. School smelled strange and sad. He sat at a desk and listened carefully.

He heard some of the names: *Charles, Ernest, Alvin, Norman, Betty, Hannah, Juliet, Viola, Polly*.

He listened carefully and heard Miss Binney say, Hannah Winter, what *are* you chewing? And he saw Hannah Winter blush. He liked Hannah Winter right from the beginning.

Gum, said Hannah.

Put it in the waste-basket, said Miss Binney.

10

He saw the little girl walk to the front of the class, take the gum from her mouth, and drop it into the waste-basket.

And he heard Miss Binney say, Ernest Gaskin, what are *you* chewing?

Gum, said Ernest.

And he liked Ernest Gaskin too.

They met in the schoolyard, and Ernest taught him a few jokes.

Amy was in the hall when school ended. She was sullen and angry at everybody until she saw the little boy. She was amazed that he wasn't changed, that he wasn't hurt, or perhaps utterly unalive, murdered. The school and everything about it frightened her very much. She took his hand and walked out of the building with him, feeling angry and proud.

Jim said, What comes after twenty-nine?

Thirty, said Amy.

Your face is dirty, he said.

His father was very quiet at the supper table.

What comes after twenty-nine? the boy said.

Thirty, said his father.

Your face is dirty, he said.

In the morning he asked his father for a nickel.

What do you want a nickel for? his father said.

Gum, he said.

His father gave him a nickel and on the way to school he stopped at Mrs Riley's store and bought a package of Spearmint.

Do you want a piece? he asked Amy.

Do you want to give me a piece? the housekeeper said.

Jim thought about it a moment, and then he said, Yes.

Do you like me? said the housekeeper.

I like you, said Jim. Do you like me?

Yes, said the housekeeper.

Do you like school?

Jim didn't know for sure, but he knew he liked the part about the gum. And Hannah Winter. And Ernest Gaskin.

I don't know, he said.

Do you sing? asked the housekeeper.

No, we don't sing, he said.

Do you play games? she said.

Not in the school, he said. In the yard we do.

He liked the part about gum very much.

Miss Binney said, Jim Davy, what are you *chewing*?

Ha ha ha, he thought.

Gum, he said.

He walked to the waste-paper basket and back to his seat, and Hannah Winter saw him, and Ernest Gaskin too. That was the best part of school.

It began to grow too.

Ernest Gaskin, he shouted in the schoolyard, *what* are you *chewing*?

Raw elephant meat, said Ernest Gaskin. Jim Davy, what are *you* chewing?

Jim tried to think of something funny to be chewing, but he couldn't.

Gum, he said, and Ernest Gaskin laughed louder than Jim laughed when Ernest Gaskin said raw elephant meat.

It was funny no matter what you said.

Going back to the classroom Jim saw Hannah Winter in the hall.

Hannah Winter, he said, *what in the world* are you *chewing*?

The little girl was startled. She wanted to say something nice that would honestly show how nice she felt about having Jim say her name and ask her the funny question, making fun of school, but she couldn't think of anything that nice to say because they were almost in the room and there wasn't time enough.

Tutti-frutti, she said with desperate haste.

It seemed to Jim he had never before heard such a glorious word, and he kept repeating the word to himself all day.

Tutti-frutti, he said to Amy on the way home.

Amy Larson, he said, *what, are, you, chewing*?

He told his father all about it at the supper table.

He said, Once there was a hill. On the hill there was a mill. Under the mill there was a walk. Under the walk there was a key. What is it?

I don't know, his father said. What is it?

Milwaukee, said the boy.

The housekeeper was delighted.

Mill. Walk. Key, Jim said.

Tutti-frutti.

What's that? said his father.

Gum, he said. The kind Hannah Winter chews.

Who's Hannah Winter? said his father.

She's in my room, he said.

Oh, said his father.

After supper he sat on the floor with the small red and blue and yellow top that hummed while it spinned. It was all right, he guessed. It was still very sad, but the gum part of it was very funny and the Hannah Winter part very nice. Raw elephant meat, he thought with great inward delight.

Raw elephant meat, he said aloud to his father who was reading the evening paper. His father folded the paper and sat on the floor beside him.

The housekeeper saw them together on the floor and for some reason tears came to her eyes.

Starting points

1. *Talk about your own first day at school (or at a new school). What happened and how did you feel?*

2. *Write your own story about a funny incident at your present school. It can be wholly true, based partly on a real incident or completely invented.*

3. *Working in a small group, prepare a radio-play version of the scenes of gum-chewing in the classroom. You might like to use footsteps and other sound effects as well as voices.*

4. *Look back over the story at all the adults Jim comes into contact with. Decide which one of them understands the boy best and try to say why.*

WHAT THE NEIGHBOURS DID

Philippa Pearce

MUM didn't like the neighbours, although – as we were the end cottage of the row – we only had one, really: Dirty Dick. Beyond him, the Macys.

Dick lived by himself – they said there used to be a wife, but she'd run away years ago; so now he lived as he wanted, which Mum said was like a pig in a pig-sty. Once I told Mum that I envied him, and she blew me up for it. Anyway, I'd have liked some of the things he had. He had two cars, although not for driving. He kept rabbits in one, and hens roosted in the other. He sold the eggs, which made part of his living. He made the rest from dealing in old junk (and in the village they said that he'd a stocking full of gold sovereigns which he kept under the mattress of his bed). Mostly he went about on foot, with his handcart for the junk; but he also rode a tricycle. The boys used to jeer at him sometimes, and once I asked him why he didn't ride a bicycle like everyone else. He said he liked a tricycle because you could go as slowly as you wanted, looking at things properly, without ever falling off.

Mrs Macy didn't like Dirty Dick any more than my Mum did, but then she disliked everybody anyway. She didn't like Mr Macy. He was retired, and every morning in all weathers Mrs Macy'd turn him out into the garden and lock the door against him and make him stay there until he'd done as much work as she thought right. She'd put his dinner out to him through the scullery window. She couldn't bear to have anything alive about the place (you couldn't count old Macy himself, Dad used to say). That was one of the reasons why she didn't think much of us, with our dog and cat and Nora's two love-birds in a cage. Dirty Dick's hens and rabbits were even worse, of course.

14

Then the affair of the yellow dog made the Macys really hate Dirty Dick. It seems that old Mr Macy secretly got himself a dog. He never had any money of his own, because his wife made him hand it over, every week; so Dad reckoned that he must have begged the dog off someone who'd otherwise have had it destroyed.

The dog began as a secret, which sounds just about impossible, with Mrs Macy around. But every day Mr Macy used to take his dinner and eat it in his tool-shed, which opened on the side furthest from the house. That must have been his temptation; but none of us knew he'd fallen into it, until one summer evening we heard a most awful screeching from the Macys' house.

'That's old Ma Macy screaming,' said Dad, spreading his bread and butter.

'Oh, dear!' said Mum, jumping up and then sitting down again. 'Poor old Mr Macy!' But Mum was afraid of Mrs Macy. 'Run upstairs, boy, and see if you can see what's going on.'

So I did. I was just in time for the excitement, for, as I leaned out of the window, the Macys' back door flew open. Mr Macy came out first, with his head down and his arms sort of curved above it; and Mrs Macy came out close behind him, aiming at his head with a light broom – but aiming quite hard. She was screeching words, although it was difficult to pick out any of them. But some words came again and again, and I began to follow: Mr Macy had brought hairs with him into the house – short, curly, yellowish hairs, and he'd left those hairs all over the upholstery, and they must have come from a cat or a dog or a hamster or I don't know what, and so on and so on. Whatever the creature was, he'd been keeping it in the tool-shed, and turn it out he was going to, this very minute.

As usual, Mrs Macy was right about what Mr Macy was going to do.

He opened the shed door and out ambled a dog – a big, yellowy-white old dog, looking a bit like a sheep, somehow, and about as quick-witted. As though it didn't notice what a tantrum Mrs Macy was in, it blundered gently towards her, and she lifted her broom high, and Mr Macy covered his eyes; and then Mrs Macy let out a real scream – a plain shriek – and dropped the broom and shot indoors and slammed the door after her.

The dog seemed puzzled, naturally; and so was I. It lumbered around towards Mr Macy, and then I saw its head properly, and that it had the most extraordinary eyes – like headlamps, somehow. I don't mean as big as headlamps, of course, but with a kind of whitish glare to them. Then I realized that the poor old thing must be blind.

The dog had raised its nose inquiringly towards Mr Macy, and Mr Macy had taken one timid, hopeful step towards the dog, when one of the sash-windows of the house went up and Mrs Macy leaned out. She'd recovered from her panic, and she gave Mr Macy his orders. He was to take that disgusting animal and turn it out into the road, where he must have found it in the first place.

I knew that old Macy would be too dead scared to do anything else but what his wife told him.

I went down again to where the others were having tea.

'Well?' said Mum.

I told them, and I told them what Mrs Macy was making Mr Macy do to the blind dog. 'And if it's turned out like that on the road, it'll be killed by the first car that comes along.'

There was a pause, when even Nora seemed to be thinking; but I could see from their faces what they were thinking.

Dad said at last: 'That's bad. But we've four people in this little house, and a dog already, and a cat and two birds. There's no room for anything else.'

'But it'll be killed.'

'No,' said Dad. 'Not if you go at once, before any car comes, and take that dog down to the village, to the police station. Tell them it's a stray.'

'But what'll they do with it?'

Dad looked as though he wished I hadn't asked that, but he said: 'Nothing, I expect. Well, they might hand it over to the Cruelty to Animals people.'

'And what'll *they* do with it?'

Dad was rattled. 'They do what they think best for animals – I should have thought they'd have taught you that at school. For goodness sake, boy!'

Dad wasn't going to say any more, nor Mum, who'd been listening with her lips pursed up. But everyone knew that the most likely thing was that an old, blind, ownerless dog would be destroyed.

But anything would be better than being run over and killed by a car just as you were sauntering along in the evening sunlight; so I started out of the house after the dog.

There he was, sauntering along, just as I'd imagined him. No

16

sign of Mr Macy, of course: he'd have been called back indoors by his wife.

As I ran to catch up with the dog, I saw Dirty Dick coming home, and nearer the dog than I was. He was pushing his handcart, loaded with the usual bits of wood and other junk. He saw the dog coming and stopped, and waited; the dog came on hesitantly towards him.

'I'm coming for him,' I called.

'Ah,' said Dirty Dick. 'Yours?' He held out his hand towards the dog – the hand that my mother always said she could only bear to take hold of if the owner had to be pulled from certain death in a quicksand. Anyway, the dog couldn't see the colour of it, and it positively seemed to like the smell; it came on.

'No,' I said. 'Macys were keeping it, but Mrs Macy turned it out. I'm going to take it down to the police as a stray. What do you think they'll do with it?'

Dirty Dick never said much; this time he didn't answer. He just bent down to get his arm round the dog and in a second he'd hoisted him up on top of all the stuff in the cart. Then he picked up the handles and started off again.

So the Macys saw the blind dog come back to the row of cottages in state, as you might say, sitting on top of half a broken lava-tory-seat on the very pinnacle of Dirty Dick's latest load of junk.

Dirty Dick took good care of his animals, and he took good care of this dog he adopted. It always looked well-fed and well-brushed. Sometimes he'd take it out with him, on the end of a long string; mostly he'd leave it comfortably at home. When it lay out in the back garden, old Mr Macy used to look at it longingly over the fence. Once or twice I saw him poke his fingers through, towards what had once been *his* dog. But that had been for only a very short, dark time in the shed; and the old dog never moved towards the fingers. Then 'Macy!' his terrible old wife would call from the house, and he'd have to go.

Then suddenly we heard that Dirty Dick had been robbed – old Macy came round specially to tell us. 'An old sock stuffed with pound notes, that he kept up the bedroom chimney. Gone. Hasn't he *told* you?'

'No,' said Mum, 'but we don't have a lot to do with him.' She might have added that we didn't have a lot to do with the Macys either – I think this was the first time I'd ever seen one step over our threshold in a neighbourly way.

17

'You're thick with him sometimes,' said old Macy, turning on me. 'Hasn't he told *you* all about it?'

'Me?' I said. 'No.'

'Mind you, the whole thing's not to be wondered at,' said the old man. 'Front and back doors never locked, and money kept in the house. That's a terrible temptation to anyone with a weakness that way. A temptation that shouldn't have been put.'

'I daresay,' said Mum. 'It's a shame, all the same. His savings.'

'Perhaps the police'll be able to get it back for him,' I said. 'There'll be clues.'

The old man jumped – a nervous sort of jump. 'Clues? You think the police will find clues? I never thought of that. No, I did not. But has he gone to the police, anyway, I wonder. That's what I wonder. That's what I'm asking you.' He paused, and I realized that he meant me again. 'You're thick with him, boy. Has he gone to the police? That's what I want to know.... '

His mouth seemed to have filled with saliva, so that he had to stop to swallow, and couldn't say more. He was in a state, all right.

At that moment Dad walked in from work and wasn't best pleased to find that visitor instead of his tea waiting; and Mr Macy went.

Dad listened to the story over tea, and across the fence that evening he spoke to Dirty Dick and said he was sorry to hear about the money.

'Who told you?' asked Dirty Dick.

Dad said that old Macy had told us. Dirty Dick just nodded; he didn't seem interested in talking about it any more. Over that week-end no police came to the row, and you might have thought that old Macy had invented the whole thing, except that Dirty Dick had not contradicted him.

On Monday I was rushing off to school when I saw Mr Macy in their front garden, standing just between a big laurel bush and the fence. He looked straight at me and said 'Good morning' in a kind of whisper. I don't know which was odder – the whisper, or his wishing me good morning. I answered in rather a shout, because I was late and hurrying past. His mouth had opened as though he meant to say more, but then it shut, as though he'd changed his mind. That was all, that morning.

The next morning he was in just the same spot again, and hailed me in the same way; and this time I was early, so I stopped.

He was looking shiftily about him, as though someone might be spying on us; but at least his wife couldn't be doing that, because the laurel bush was between him and their front windows. There was a tiny pile of yellow froth at one corner of his mouth, as though he'd been chewing his words over in advance. The sight of the froth made me want not to stay; but then the way he looked at me made me feel that I had to. No, it just made me; I had to.

'Look what's turned up in our back garden,' he said, in the same whispering voice. And he held up a sock so dirty – partly with soot – and so smelly that it could only have been Dirty Dick's. It was stuffed full of something – pound notes, in fact. Old Macy's story of the robbery had been true in every detail.

I gaped at him.

'It's all to go back,' said Mr Macy. 'Back exactly to where it came from.' And then, as though I'd suggested the obvious – that he should hand the sock back to Dirty Dick himself with the same explanation just given to me: 'No, no. It must go back as though it had never been – never been taken away.' He couldn't use the word 'stolen'. 'Mustn't have the police poking round us. Mrs Macy wouldn't like it.' His face twitched at his own mention of her; he leaned forward. 'You must put it back, boy. Put it back for me and keep your mouth shut. Go on. Yes.'

He must have been half out of his mind to think that I should do it, especially as I still didn't twig why. But as I stared at his twitching face I suddenly did understand. I mean, that old Macy had taken the sock, out of spite, and then lost his nerve.

He must have been half out of his mind to think that I would do that for him; and yet I did it. I took the sock and put it inside my jacket and turned back to Dirty Dick's cottage. I walked boldly up to the front door and knocked, and of course there was no answer. I knew he was already out with the cart.

There wasn't a sign of anyone looking, either from our house or the Macys'. (Mr Macy had already disappeared.) I tried the door and it opened, as I knew it would. I stepped inside and closed it behind me.

I'd never been inside before. The house was dirty, I suppose, and smelt a bit, but not really badly. It smelt of Dirty Dick and hens and rabbits – although it was untrue that he kept either hens or rabbits indoors, as Mrs Macy said. It smelt of dog, too, of course.

Opening straight off the living-room, where I stood, was the twisty, dark little stairway – exactly as in our cottage next door.

I went up.

The first room upstairs was full of junk. A narrow passageway had been kept clear to the second room, which opened off the first one. This was Dirty Dick's bedroom, with the bed unmade, as it probably was for weeks on end.

There was the fire-place, too, with a good deal of soot which had recently been brought down from the chimney. You couldn't miss seeing that – Dirty Dick couldn't have missed it, at the time. Yet he'd done nothing about his theft. In fact, I realized now that he'd probably said nothing either. The only person who'd let the cat out of the bag was poor old Macy himself.

I'd been working this out as I looked at the fire-place, standing quite still. Round me the house was silent. The only sound came from outside, where I could see a hen perched on the bumper of the old car in the back garden, clucking for an egg newly laid. But when she stopped, there came another, tiny sound that terrified me: the click of a front gate opening. Feet were clumping up to the front door....

I stuffed the sock up the chimney again, any old how, and was out of that bedroom in seconds; but on the threshold of the junk-room I stopped, fixed by the headlamp glare of the old blind dog. He must have been there all the time, lying under a three-legged washstand, on a heap of rags. All the time he would have been watching me, if he'd had his eyesight. He didn't move.

Meanwhile the front door had opened and the footsteps had clumped inside, and stopped. There was a long pause, while I stared at the dog, who stared at me; and down below Dirty Dick listened and waited – he must have heard my movement just before.

At last: 'Well,' he called, 'why don't you come down?'

There was nothing else to do but go. Down that dark, twisty stair, knowing that Dirty Dick was waiting for me at the bottom. He was a big man, and strong. He heaved his junk about like nobody's business.

But when I got down, he wasn't by the foot of the stairs; he was standing by the open door, looking out, with his back to me. He hadn't been surprised to hear someone upstairs in his house, uninvited; but when he turned round from the doorway, I could see that he hadn't expected to see *me*. He'd expected someone else – old Macy, I suppose.

I wanted to explain that I'd only put the sock back – there was soot all over my hands, plain to be seen, of course – and that I'd had nothing to do with taking it in the first place. But he'd drawn his thick brows together as he looked at me, and he jerked his head towards the open door. I was frightened, and I went past him without saying anything. I was late for school now, anyway, and I ran.

I didn't see Dirty Dick again.

Later that morning Mum chose to give him a talking to, over the back fence, about locking his doors against pilferers in future. She says he didn't say he would, he didn't say he wouldn't; and he didn't say anything about anything having been stolen, or returned.

Soon after that Mum saw him go out with the handcart with all his rabbits in a hutch, and he came back later without them. He did the same with his hens. We heard later that he'd given them away in the village; he hadn't even bothered to try to sell them.

Then he went round to Mum, wheeling the tricycle. He said he'd decided not to use it any more, and I could have it. He didn't leave any message for me.

Later still, Mum saw him set off for the third time that day with his handcart: not piled very high even, but with the old dog sitting on top. And that was the last that anyone saw of him.

He must have taken very little money with him: they found the sooty sock, still nearly full, by the rent-book on the mantelpiece. There was plenty to pay the rent due and to pay for cleaning up the house and the garden for the next tenant. He must have been fed up with being a householder, Dad said – and with having neighbours. He just wanted to turn tramp, and he did.

It was soon after he'd gone that I said to Mum that I envied him, and she blew me up, and went on and on about soap and water and fecklessness. All the same, I did envy him. I didn't even have the fun with his tricycle that he'd had. I never rode it, although I wanted to, because I was afraid that people I knew would laugh at me.

21

Starting points

1. *Try to decide what makes a good neighbour. Use your own experience of your own neighbours and listen to several other people's experiences and views. When you have done this, talk about all the people in the story. Decide which of them were good neighbours and why.*

2. *At the beginning and again at the end of the story the boy says he envies Dirty Dick. Look through the story again and jot down all the reasons he has to envy him. Use your notes to help you decide whether you agree with the boy and compare your opinion with other people's. Then re-write the events of the story as told by either the boy's mother or by Mr Macy or by Dirty Dick himself. Make clear the attitudes and feelings of your story-teller as you go along.*

3. *Working in pairs, talk about a time when you were blamed for something you did not do or about a time when you felt guilty about something you did (though perhaps no one else found out). Write your own story about this experience. Use your partner for help in talking over ideas and for reading and improving your version.*

4. *Working in a group of four, prepare a radio-play version of the story, starting from when Mr Macy gives the sock to the boy and ending when the boy leaves Dirty Dick's house. Use a narrator and sound effects and record your version.*

THE LION

Walter Macken

TIM stood patiently at the edge of the small crowd and waited for the appearance of the man he called Putrid in his mind.

He was a young boy. His thin hands were clasped behind his back. This was the third day he had come to watch the feeding of the animals of the circus. Tim hadn't been inside to see the circus. He could never raise the price of it, even the matinée, but the feeding of the animals was for free. Anybody could come and watch. It was a small menagerie. Just a lioness and a tiger and a few monkeys, and Samson.

Samson was the lion. It was near his cage Tim always stood. It wasn't a big cage. It barely fitted the body of the lion. Tim felt his own limbs cramped when he looked at the cage. Samson wasn't like a lion you would see in books or a picture. His mane was not bushy. It was nearly all worn away. There was only a bit of it left around his head, up near his ears. He didn't roar either. Even when he was provoked he would only loose off a sort of half-hearted growl. You know the sort of small bush that a lion has near the end of his tail. Samson didn't have that either. It was worn away. His tail was mottled, sort of mean-looking. You could see his ribs too. He wasn't a fat lion. Tim was very fond of Samson. He preferred him to the others; to the pacing tiger with the fearful eyes and to the yawning lioness. He even preferred him to the monkeys, although the monkeys were good fun.

The other children had run up to the far side of the field. There was Putrid coming out with the bucket. It was a bucket of meat. Raw meat. The sides of the bucket were stained with old blood and fresh blood. Tim felt the wave of dislike coming over him again at the sight of the man with the bucket.

He was a small man, very black-haired, always seeming to want a shave. He was carrying a pole in his hand with a steel prod on the

23

end of it. Tim felt the muscles of his stomach tightening at the sight of him. Always the same. Opening the slot in the cage of the tiger and the lioness and poking in the meat to them. He talked to those nicely enough always. They grabbed the meat and held it between their claws and squatted at the eating of it. Then he turned his face towards the cage of Samson and went into his act.

Before he could start the act, Tim turned to Samson, and he said to him: 'Don't mind him, Samson. Don't mind him. He is very ignorant.' Samson may have heard him. He turned his head towards him and blinked his great eyes, and then went back to his dreaming. Almost against his will Tim turned his eyes to watch Putrid.

There he was several yards away, crouching like an ape, the bucket in one hand, the pole in the other. The kids were around about him, laughing at his antics.

'Here's the fiercest one of them all, min,' he was saying, pointing Samson with his nose, like a dog. 'Fresh outa the jungles of Africa. Looka the red in his eyes. Watch the stretch of the claws. Oney to be approached with great caution. Careful with him now. He can stretch a limb five foot through the bars to get at ye.'

He circled around as if he was stalking. Tim watched him in disgust. He knew that the best parts would be gone from the bucket. Samson never got anything from him but the bare leavings of the others. The kids were delighted with Putrid. They started to imitate him, crouching and stalking and laughing. Suddenly Putrid darted towards the cage, inserted the prod and stuck it in Samson's side. The lion moved, almost grunting. He couldn't move far. He didn't growl. He didn't roar. Tim would have given anything to hear him roaring with anger. He didn't.

'See that,' says Putrid. 'Hear the roaring of him. Waken the dead he would. Oh, a fierce animal, kids. But, you don't have to be afraid of him. Watch this.' He left down the bucket and the pole and he ran crouching behind the cage and caught hold of Samson's tail. He pulled it as hard as he could, so that the body of the lion was pulled back to the end bars.

'See that,' he was shouting. 'The oney fierce animal in captivity to be held be the tail. He'll go mad, so he will. Watch him tear the cage to pieces.'

Tim's finger-nails were biting into his palms. Samson rose almost wearily, straightening himself, crouching because he could not stand upright in the cage, pulling against the pull on his tail, almost staggering on his pads as Putrid suddenly released him. The lion's head hit the bars on the other side. He didn't object.

Because he's old, I suppose, Tim thought. He wouldn't have done that to him when he was young. He conjured up a picture of Samson meeting Putrid in a jungle clearing. Samson wouldn't be unkind then, Tim bet. He would just tear Putrid to pieces. Tim savoured that.

Putrid rubbing his hands.

'Nothin' to it, min,' he was saying. 'I've pulled lions be the tail in every continent in the world. But this one is real fierce when he's feedin'. Oh, real fierce when he's feedin'.'

He didn't open the slot. He pulled the bar and opened the whole door of the cage. Tim wished that Samson would spring out on top of him. He didn't. Putrid hit him on the head with the prod. You could hear the sound of it. Samson just blinked his eyes and pulled back.

'No play in him at all to-day,' said Putrid. 'Here, Fanny, have your chips.' He up-ended the bucket and flung the contents of it straight into the lion's face. The lion must have looked funny with the things on his face. The bystanders were dying laughing. The scraps fell off his face then onto the floor of the cage.

Putrid banged the door and locked it.

'Bah,' he said. 'No play in him at all to-day. What a lion. Come on, we'll get to the monkeys.'

They followed him. One of them, before going, tentatively took a pull at the lion's tail which was still hanging through the bars. He let it go quickly and ran after them shouting. 'Hey, fellas, I did it. I pulled his tail.'

Putrid patted him on the head.

'Man,' he said, 'you'll be lion-tamer yet, so you will.'

They laughed.

Tim was looking at Samson.

'Maybe he doesn't mean it,' he was saying to him. 'But don't mind him. He has to die sometime and then he won't be after you.'

He felt tears in his eyes. Because I'm young, he thought. Like you would cry about a drowning kitten.

Samson started to clean his face. It took him some time. Then he sniffed at the food between his paws. It didn't interest him. He lifted his head and looked away at the sky.

At this moment Tim got the thought that maybe Samson was sick. He knew they didn't use him in the circus. Just the lioness and the tiger. They just carted him around to be a father, they said. And suddenly in his mind's eyes he saw the wood outside the town. You came down a hill to it and climbed another hill out of it, and in the hollow there was a clear stream that babbled over stones, and the wood was wide and dappled with sunlight. A place like that Samson would be at home, with the birds and the trees and the bracken, and he would get well and growl and roar and nobody would disturb him, and Putrid couldn't torture him.

On this thought, Tim reached up (he had to stretch a lot) and he pulled back the steel bolt and he opened the door of the cage.

'Come on, Samson,' he said, 'I will take you to a place that you will like. It won't be like the jungle. But it'll be nearly as good. Come on! Please come on before anybody comes.'

Samson didn't want to come.

Tim pulled himself up onto the floor of the cage until he was hanging on his chest. He stretched an arm until his hand could take hold of the remaining mane and he tugged at it gently.

'Come on, Samson,' he said. 'Come on.'

Samson resisted, but then he started to go with the pull of the boy's hand. Tim got his feet on the ground. He still kept his grip on the old lion's mane. And then Samson crouched and sprang to the earth. He stood there for a while, feeling the unaccustomed ground under his pads. Then he dutifully followed the pull of the small hand on his mane and walked beside him, past the caravans, out the gate and into the street of the town.

They walked calmly down the middle of it.

If you can ripple a pond with a pebble you can entirely upset it by throwing a large boulder into it. The pond will explode. It was like that now with the town as the first person looked at the boy and the lion.

This was a fat woman with a shopping basket. She looked and she looked again, and then she dropped her basket and opened her mouth very widely and screamed and turned and ran screaming.

Everybody claimed afterwards that it was this woman who led to the unnatural panic with her screaming. Only for her, they said, nobody would have paid the least attention to the boy and the loose lion. Perhaps, but if you are walking up a street and you see a lion walking towards you, I doubt if you will stop to ask any questions. Your skin will crawl, your mouth will dry, the hair will rise on the back of your neck and you will seek safety in flight.

26

Everybody did now. The street, thronged with people, cleared as if a plague had swept through it. People ran into the first open shop door, fighting to get in and to bang the doors behind them, and peer out through the glass. Screaming women and shouting men, all panic-stricken. They ran into cars and closed the doors of them and shot up the windows of them, and peered palely through them.

Tim walked solemnly on, talking to Samson, almost unconscious of the confusion and upset he was leaving behind him. He turned from the busy shopping and market street into the wide Square. This was roomier and people had more time to find safety and to reflect.

Tim paused at the top of the Square and became aware of all the disturbance he was causing and also became aware of the line of police gradually and very cautiously closing in on him. His hand tightened on Samson, and he stopped, and Samson stopped and looked at the circle of men approaching him. He raised a lip and snarled, and the advancing line came to a dead stop, all except the Inspector, a tall man with blue eyes, who came close to the boy and the lion with nothing under his arm except a light cane. He had sense. He had called the circus people. Out of one corner of his eye he saw them approaching now, out of the street into the Square, loaded with ropes and bars and hauling a cage on wheels which they lifted down from a van.

'Take it easy, boy,' said the Inspector. 'Don't get excited. Nothing will happen. Don't excite him.'

Tim's mouth was dry. He suddenly realized that his hopes were at an end. He hadn't thought of the town and the police. If he could have gone a back way, nobody might have noticed. Now, he thought sadly, Samson would never see the wood.

The Inspector was surprised as he closed on him. The boy had no fear, and as he looked closely at the lion, he saw there was no need for anybody to fear. All the same, who knew? The lion looked old and thin and helpless, but one slash at the boy was all that was needed.

The men were closing from behind, cautiously, the ropes held in loops.

'Leave the lion and come here to me,' said the Inspector.

Tim shook his head.

'No, no,' he said, his small hand tightening on the lion.

'You'll have to leave him go,' said the Inspector. 'The men are behind you. They are going to throw ropes over him. You'll have to come to me.'

'Don't let Putrid touch him,' said Tim.

The Inspector didn't know what he was talking about.

'All right,' he said.

'Good-bye Samson,' said Tim then, pressing his hand deeply into the lion's neck. He didn't look at him any more. He bent his head and walked to the Inspector. The Inspector heaved a sigh and caught his hand. He watched for a short time as the ropes landed, and the lion was secured. Like a pent-up breath relieved, there was laughter and calling and shouting. He noticed the small, black, dirty little fellow cavorting around the lion as they put him into the cage. He went docilely, peacefully. But this chap was acting the mickey for the surrounding people. And they were laughing at his antics.

'All right,' said the Inspector, 'let's go down and get off the streets and see what this is all about.'

Tim soon found himself alone in a small room with just a desk and a bright fire, and the Inspector who didn't seem so tall when he was sitting down.

'Now, Tim,' he said, 'tell me. Did you open the cage?'

'Yes, sir,' said Tim.

'Why?' he asked.

'I wanted to bring him out to the woods,' Tim said. 'So that he would get well, and Putrid wouldn't torture him.'

Tim told him about Putrid.

'I see,' said the Inspector.

'Samson is not well,' said Tim. 'You should have seen him. He wouldn't roar nor nothing. And he should have. He should have eaten Putrid. But he didn't do nothing. Just sat when he stuck things into him and pulled his tail and everything. You see, Samson should be in the woods to get well.'

'I see,' said the Inspector. He took up the telephone and called a number into it. He tapped with a pencil on the desk as he waited. His eyes were hard. Tim was frightened again.

'That you, Joe?' he asked. 'Yes, it's me. I want you down here in about ten minutes. Bring your bag of tricks with you. Yes, I'll explain to you then. It's urgent.'

He put down the phone. He pressed a button and started to write lines on a sheet of paper. Another policeman came in.

'Here,' he said. 'Go to the J.P. down the road and get him to sign that.' The policeman went.

'All right, Tim,' said the Inspector, 'come on and we'll go out and wait for Joe.'

'What are you going to do with me?' Tim asked. 'Will I have to go to jail?'

The Inspector looked at him for a moment, then put his hand on his head.

'No, Tim,' he said. 'No jail. On the other hand, no medal either. They don't give out medals for the kind of good deed you do. Come on.' They went out. The Inspector opened the door of a car and put Tim in before him. There was a bulky red-faced man behind the wheel.

'Hello, Joe,' said the Inspector. 'This is Tim, a friend of mine.'

'Hello, Tim,' said Joe. 'Glad the Inspector has decent friends for a change.'

The policeman came breathless then, shoved in the paper through the window.

'He made no trouble about it?' the Inspector asked.

'Not a bit,' said the policeman, laughing. 'Said he'd sign an order to burn the circus as well.'

The Inspector laughed.

'Fine. All right, Joe.'

The car moved away.

'What's all this about a lion?' Joe asked. 'Everybody is talking about it.'

'That's the lion you are going to see,' said the Inspector. He explained to Tim. 'Joe is a doctor of animals, Tim. He cares for animals, like a doctor cares for people.'

Tim was interested.

'Oh,' he said. 'Will you make Samson well?'

'He will, Tim, don't worry,' said the Inspector.

Joe was a bit bewildered, but kept silent under the appeal of the Inspector's wink.

The car stopped outside the circus entrance. The town had returned to normal.

'You stay here, Tim,' said the Inspector. 'We won't be long.'

They left him. Tim opened a window. He could smell the circus. He didn't want to go in there again.

Joe was looking at Samson.

'What do you think?' the Inspector asked.

'I'm afraid so,' said Joe.

'You wait here,' said the Inspector.

He found the owner. He presented him with the signed order.

'You can't do that,' he protested. 'It's illegal. There's nothing wrong with him. Just because some crazy kid let him out. That's no reason. Here, Alphonsus. Come here. He knows. He keeps them fed. You know that Samson is all right, isn't he? Isn't Samson all right?'

'Strong as a lion,' said Alphonsus, chuckling.

'You are Putrid,' said the Inspector suddenly to Alphonsus. He thought how vivid had been the boy's description of him. 'You're a dirty little sadistic bastard,' he said, 'and if a lion doesn't tear you to pieces some day, some honest man will kick your puddens out.'

Putrid's mouth was open in astonishment.

The owner protested.

'Here,' he said. 'You can't say things like that.'

'You keep that fella away from your animals,' said the Inspector and walked away from them.

Joe was at the cage. He was putting away a syringe. Samson was lying on the floor of the cage, his legs stiffened straight out from him. His chest was not rising.

They looked at the body of the lion.

'He should have been destroyed years ago,' Joe said.

'Poor devil,' said the Inspector. He put his hand through the bars of the cage, rested it on the body of Samson.

'That's from Tim, Samson,' he said, and then they walked back to the car. They got in.

They could sense the silence of the boy.

'What happened?' he asked.

Joe started the car.

The Inspector put his arm around Tim's shoulders.

'Samson is gone back to the woods, Tim,' he said. 'You watch. One time maybe when you are playing in that wood, you might see Samson standing in the sunlight.'

'Resting on the soft leaves,' said Tim eagerly.

'That's right,' said the Inspector.

Starting points

1. Using the story as your starting point, talk in a small group about the way animals are used for entertainment and of any occasion when you have seen ill-treatment.

2. Look back over the story and jot down phrases which describe Putrid, how he looks, behaves and feels. Re-write the story from Putrid's viewpoint.

3. Imagine that you are an inspector for the RSPCA (Royal Society for the Prevention of Cruelty to Animals). Paying close attention to details in the story, write your report on Samson.

4. Re-read the story up to the point where Tim opens the door of the cage. In groups of five or six, act out this part of the story, trying to make clear the different attitudes of Tim and Putrid to the feeding of Samson.

MOTHER AND SON

Liam O'Flaherty

ALTHOUGH it was only five o'clock, the sun had already set and the evening was very still, as all spring evenings are, just before the birds begin to sing themselves to sleep; or maybe tell one another bedside stories. The village was quiet. The men had gone away to fish for the night after working all the morning with the sowing. Women were away milking the cows in the little fields among the crags.

Brigid Gill was alone in her cottage waiting for her son to come home from school. He was now an hour late, and as he was only nine she was very nervous about him especially as he was her only child and he was a wild boy always getting into mischief, mitching from school, fishing minnows on Sunday and building stone 'castles' in the great crag above the village. She kept telling herself that she would give him a good scolding and beating when he came in, but at the same time her heart was thumping with anxiety and she started at every sound, rushing out to the door and looking down the winding road, that was now dim with the shadows of the evening. So many things could happen to a little boy.

His dinner of dried fish and roast potatoes was being kept warm in the oven among the peat ashes beside the fire on the hearth, and on the table there was a plate, a knife and a little mug full of buttermilk.

At last she heard the glad cries of the schoolboys afar off, and rushing out she saw them scampering, not up the road, but across the crags to the left, their caps in their hands.

'Thank God,' she said, and then she persuaded herself that she was very angry. Hurriedly she got a small dried willow rod, sat down on a chair within the door and waited for Stephen.

He advanced up the yard very slowly, walking near the stone fence that bounded the vegetable garden, holding his satchel in his left hand by his side, with his cap in his right hand, a red-cheeked slim boy, dressed in close-fitting grey frieze trousers that reached a little below his knees and a blue sweater. His feet were bare and covered with all sorts of mud. His face perspired and his great soft blue eyes were popping out of his head with fright. He knew his mother would be angry.

At last he reached the door and, holding down his head, he entered the kitchen. The mother immediately jumped up and seized him by the shoulder. The boy screamed, dropped his satchel and his cap and clung to her apron. The mother raised the rod to strike, but when she looked down at the trembling body, she began to tremble herself and dropped the stick. Stooping down, she raised him up and began kissing him, crying at the same time with tears in her eyes.

'What's going to become of you at all, at all? God save us, I haven't the courage to beat you and you're breaking my heart with your wickedness.'

The boy sobbed, hiding his head in his mother's bosom.

'Go away,' she said, thrusting him away from her, 'and eat your dinner. Your father will give to you a good thrashing in the morning. I've spared you often and begged him not to beat you, but this time I'm not going to say a word for you. You've my heart broken, so you have. Come here and eat your dinner.'

She put the dinner on the plate and pushed the boy into the chair. He sat down sobbing, but presently he wiped his eyes with his sleeve and began to eat ravenously. Gradually his face brightened and he moved about on the chair, settling himself more comfortably and forgetting all his fears of his mother and the thrashing he was going to get next morning in the joy of satisfying his hunger. The mother sat on the doorstep, knitting in silence and watching him lovingly from under her long black eyelashes.

All her anger had vanished by now and she felt glad that she had thrust all the responsibility for punishment on to her husband. Still, she wanted to be severe, and although she wanted to ask Stephen what he had been doing, she tried to hold her tongue. At last, however, she had to talk.

'What kept you, Stephen?' she said softly.

Stephen swallowed the last mouthful and turned around with his mug in his hand.

'We were only playing ball,' he said excitedly, 'and then Red Michael ran after us and chased us out of his field where we were playing. And we had to run an awful way; oh, a long, long way we had to run, over crags where I never was before.'

'But didn't I often tell you not to go into people's fields to play ball?'

'Oh, mother, sure it wasn't me but the other boys that wanted to go, and if I didn't go with them they'd say I was afraid, and father says I mustn't be afraid.'

'Yes, you pay heed to your father but you pay no heed to your mother that has all the trouble with you. Now and what would I do if you fell running over the crags and sprained your ankle?'

And she put her apron to her eyes to wipe away a tear.

Stephen left his chair, came over to her and put his arms around her neck.

'Mother,' he said, 'I'll tell you what I saw on the crags if you promise not to tell father about me being late and playing ball in Red Michael's field.'

'I'll do no such thing,' she said.

'Oh, do, mother,' he said, 'and I'll never be late again, never, never, never.'

'All right, Stephen; what did you see, my little treasure?'

He sat down beside her on the threshold and, looking wistfully out into the sky, his eyes became big and dreamy and his face assumed an expression of mystery and wonder.

'I saw a great big black horse,' he said, 'running in the sky over our heads, but none of the other boys saw it but me, and I didn't tell them about it. The horse had seven tails and three heads and its belly was so big you could put our house into it. I saw it with my two eyes. I did, mother. And then it soared and galloped away, away, ever so far. Isn't that a great thing I saw, mother?'

'It is, darling,' she said dreamily, looking out into the sky, thinking of something with soft eyes. There was silence. Then Stephen spoke again without looking at her.

'Sure you won't tell on me, mother?'

'No, treasure, I won't.'

'On your soul you won't?'

'Hush! little one. Listen to the birds. They are beginning to sing. I won't tell at all. Listen to the beautiful ones.'

They both sat in silence, listening and dreaming, both of them.

34

Starting points

1. *Talk about a time you came in late. How did you feel? What did people at home say and do? How do you think they felt?*

2. *Look back and find how Mrs Gill feels about her son at different stages in the story. Why do you think she feels as she does?*

3. *Write in more detail the part of the story from when Stephen leaves school to the time Red Michael chases the boys out of his field. Tell the story from Stephen's point of view.*

4. *Working in threes, prepare a script of the scene and conversation when Michael's father comes home. Try out your scene and if possible record it.*

THE TREE

J.C. Badcock

WE were returning home, in the spring's early light-fade, from the old brickyard; returning through the spongy turf-meadows, and the new grass was kind to the feet and soft as down. We had vaulted gates, climbed trees to the very tops, jumped across streams normally too wide to be cleared, and raced over the carpet of turf, shouting madly at nothing.

But we had sobered down now and were homeward bound. 'Hark! Wha's that?' said Brad, and stopped abruptly. 'Thought I heard a shout.' I listened intently.

'There's a jinny-wren chackering in the top hedge,' I hazarded. 'T'aint that,' Brad replied. 'It's a somebody not a something. Hark!'

From the distance, over the brown rise of the hill that lay ahead, a shrill voice called:

'O – oh! Muther! Muther!' and there was something akin to terror in the cry that rose to a shriek at the end.

I felt the hair lift on the back of my head and goose-flesh pimples come to my arms.

Brad stood for a moment as though turned to stone, then swiftly gripped my arm. 'Come on,' he gasped. 'There's someone in the pit at Top Langle.'

Two broad fields separated us from the ploughland, from which direction the cries appeared to come, and over these we raced. Over the lichen-covered fence, soft-rotten with age, that cracked and collapsed under our weight; over the next field-gate whose top bar had a strand of barbed wire coiled neatly round it. In our haste we were not conscious of the barbs that tore at our legs as we half-fell over the obstacle.

The pit was hidden from our view by the tall hedge that bordered it on the side from which we were approaching, and we ran blindly, without knowing what we were to find, for now the cries had ceased and there was an eerie silence except for our own heavy breathing. We burst through the hedge and on to the pit-bank, almost scaring the life out of a water-hen that had been sorting amongst the duckweed in the middle of the pond.

In the middle of the pond? Brad and I looked at each other blankly, and not without relief.

'Well,' said my brother, 'he ain't here, and that's a good job.'

I nodded in agreement. 'But where the deuce –?'

We were interrupted by a low whimpering sound that seemed to come from the two tall elm trees in whose shade we were standing. Brad looked sharply upwards, and, before my eyes could follow his, he had suddenly collapsed on the grass in a paroxysm of laughter which left him almost speechless for moments.

'What is it?' I asked, half-angrily, not being allowed to share the joke, yet full of laughter myself, in the knowledge that my enlightenment was to come.

'Oh, dear!' gasped Brad. 'Oh, dear! The tree – the tree!'

As I gazed into the upper branches of the elm, the laughter died in my throat, for there, some forty feet up, was the deathly white face of a boy of about my own age, looking down at us in terror. His body was lying flat along a branch of the tree that stretched at right-angles from the trunk, and his weight had bent down the bough until his head was slightly lower than the rest of his body, and, but for his panic-stricken hold, he must surely have fallen to his death in the meadow below.

In the smaller twigs at the end of the bough was an assortment of odds and ends of sticks and dead leaves from the previous year, which, accidentally gathered into some semblance of a shape, had misled the unfortunate lad into thinking that it was perhaps a ring-dove's nest. His attempt to 'rag' the 'nest' had got him into a serious position.

I shook Brad to his feet.

'Can't you see – ' I began indignantly.

'I know,' he gulped hilariously, 'but I can't help it. I can't stop.'

I jumped for the lower branch and missed it.

'Give me a leg-up,' I demanded. Brad obeyed, and soon I was on his shoulders. They were still convulsed with spasms of laughter.

I climbed rapidly among the lower branches of the elm.

It was an easy journey upwards, with wens and bark-breaks every few feet, and hand-holds of waterwood between the outshoots of the branches. I found a finger-grip in the hole of the green woodpecker's nest – and a toe-stand on the rough surface of the lichen-covered bark.

In spite of the terror-distorted features, I had recognised the 'treed' lad as young Theon, a village boy who had gained some distinction as a scholar, and who was, in consequence, a favourite with the schoolmasters. 'The showpiece,' we called him.

As I drew near to the branch upon which Theon was so precariously perched, I called to him:

'Hold on, there. You're all right, you know. Just you hold on.'

'Yes,' came back the answer. 'Yes. I'm glad you've come. I'm so afraid.'

'You 'otch yourself back'ards,' I suggested, giving instructions. 'Push yourself off with your hands and slide your behind back to the tree-trunk.'

'I daren't. I'm afraid,' came the tremulous reply.

I looked down at Brad, standing under the tree. He appeared a long way away.

'Can't you manage him?' he yelled through cupped hands.

'He won't move!' I shouted back. 'He's too frit,' with a grin. 'I'm going along for him.'

Brad slapped his knees with joy.

I eased my way round the thinning main trunk of the elm, and, throwing my leg over the branch upon which the boy lay, sat astride, facing his direction.

'You're all right,' I reassured. 'Don't you worry. You'll be all right.'

My progress towards him, over the horizontal bough, was in a series of forward jerks which at first were unnoticed by him, but, as the branch became thinner, there was a slight swaying which completely terrified him.

And, as I got nearer, the combined weight of the two of us had an almost disastrous effect.

There was a sudden downward bending of the springy bough, and a scream from Theon. I flattened myself on the branch immediately I felt the motion, winding both legs around its rough circumference, grabbing, at the same time, the thick corduroy trousers of the now almost fainting boy.

'Shut your eyes,' I cried. 'Don't look down. Hang on. I've got you. Steady up now, or you'll have us both off.'

His coat-flaps peeled up his back and covered his head, and things fell from his pockets; a penknife; a few stones; a pencil-stub;

a fine morocco purse that spun in the air and took a long time to reach the ground. And thus we lay for some moments, he, a complete victim of his fright, and I, in a more favourable position than he, trying to conquer mine.

Brad had seen our plight, and the fun went out of his heart. Like a monkey, he was in the tree, leaping prodigiously to clutch the bottom starting-branch, climbing with feet and finger-tips where the internodes were longest, up to the very branch upon which we were marooned, and to the bough above, from where he looked down at us.

He lay dangerously over in an attempt to help us, but we were out of his reach.

'Don't come down on to this branch,' I warned.

I began to talk to Theon, telling him to release his hold, hand at a time, and to ' 'otch' himself backwards as I steadied him.

'Sit upright,' I said. 'You won't fall. I'm holding you,' but he could only whimper and clutch more tightly at his frail link with life. For he could see only the danger ahead; safety lay behind him.

'Leave loose,' I urged. 'Leave loose.' With one hand I punched at his ribs, pulling at him with the other, but the action made the bough dip and lift, and he screamed, and hung on the tighter. I turned my head sideways, and looked at Brad hopelessly.

'He won't let go,' I said, unnecessarily.

Brad thought for a moment. He was worried.

'Rest for a bit,' he said, and I was glad of the chance.

The mental strain was as great as the physical, for whilst I was pulling my strength away at the terrified Theon, fear was tugging away at me, and with a deal more success. I looked again at Brad, and, to my indignation, found him sitting comfortably astride his perch, hacking, with his jack-knife, at a long whippy elm-cane which he had cut.

He saw my questioning stare.

'Get a grip on him,' he said grimly, 'and be ready to pull.' Then, leaning over, he thrashed at Theon's hands, time and time again, until the thin, white knuckles became pink and, as the flaying went on, the taut skin broke, red with the thin smear of blood. Under this desperate pressure the boy released his vice-like grip, and I could feel some of the tension leave his body. At that moment I pulled him backwards so abruptly that the effort almost unseated us both.

'Steady,' snarled Brad.

Although Theon had come back but a couple of feet, it had been sufficient to ease the weight on the end of the branch, and as I worked my way gently backwards to a similar distance the feather twigs at the end of the bough lifted again and hid from our view the ground below.

'You're all right now,' I murmured to the lad. 'Just move your hands back a bit.' To emphasise my words, Brad cut him again across the knuckles. Theon yelled, but there was anger in his cry now, and he drew away his hands towards his body until he was sitting almost upright, and from this position, with infinite care, he was edged, inch by inch, towards the thick, main trunk of the tree.

'All right?' queried Brad from above, as we stood on the stout branch near its junction, both a little breathless.

'Yes,' answered Theon. 'I say – ' he began.

Brad cut him short.

'Get down,' he commanded. To me, 'You go first and watch this fool's feet.'

It was easy going. The boy had lost his fright now that he could place hands and feet on solid branches which did not sway and terrify, and he came to the grass without further help. Brad, who had been watching our progress from high up in the tree, came down like a tornado, swinging from the lowest branch and landing on all fours by our side. His eyes were rather red and staring, and there was a slight flush high up on his cheeks.

He turned on Theon in a fury.

'Keep out of trees, you, boy. Now go home.'

The lad clasped my hand and I felt suddenly foolish, and looked down at the worn toes of my boots.

'Thank you,' he said quietly, 'I don't know what I'd have done.'

Brad snarled.

'You,' he said, 'who cares about you?'

As we went homewards towards the village, the partridges were creaking in the Mill Hill ploughland – for it was near evening, the time when they speak to each other from the corners of the fields – but we walked in silence.

Starting points

1. *Note down the way Brad's feelings change throughout the story. Use your notes to talk in a small group about why he feels and acts in the way he does.*

2. *Re-tell the story from the point of view of Theon, the boy in the tree.*

3. *Talk about a time when you were afraid or when someone you know behaved in a cowardly or a cruel way. Use your incident as the basis for your own short story.*

4. *Talk in a small group about the relationship between the two brothers. How does it alter in the story and why? Work together on a play script which contains an event that affects the relationship between two friends or between two relatives. Rehearse your play and try it out for others in your class.*

POWER

Jack Cope

FROM the gum tree at the corner he looked out over, well –
nothing. There was nothing more after his father's place, only the
veld, so flat and unchanging that the single shadowy koppie away
off towards the skyline made it look more empty still. It was a
lonely koppie like himself.

The one thing that made a difference was the powerline. High
above the earth on its giant steel lattice towers, the powerline
strode across the veld until it disappeared beyond the koppie.

It passed close to his father's place and one of the great pylons
was on their ground, in a square patch fenced off with barbed wire,
a forbidden place. André used to look through the wire at the
pylon. Around the steelwork itself were more screens of barbed
wire and on all four sides of it enamel warning-plates with a red
skull-and-crossbones said in three languages, DANGER! and there
was a huge figure of volts, millions of volts.

André was ten and he knew volts were electricity and the line
took power by a short cut far across country. It worked gold mines,
it lit towns, and hauled trains and drove machinery somewhere
out beyond. The power-station was in the town ten miles on the
other side of his father's place and the great line simply jumped
right over them without stopping.

He used to lie and listen to the marvellous hum of the powerline,
the millions of volts flowing invisible and beyond all one's ideas
along the copper wires that hung so smooth and light from ties of
crinkled white china looking like Chinese lanterns up against the
sky. Faint cracklings and murmurs and rushes of sound would
sometimes come from the powerline, and at night he was sure he
saw soft blue flames lapping and trembling on the wires as if they

42

were only half peeping out of that fierce river of volts. The flames danced and their voices chattered to him of a mystery.

He loved the powerline dearly. It made a door through the distance for his thoughts. It was like him except that it never slept, and while he was dreaming it went on without stopping, crackling faintly and murmuring. Its electricity hauled up the mine skips from the heart of the earth, hurtled huge green rail units along their shining lines, and thundered day and night in the factories.

Now that the clear warm autumn days were coming after the summer thunderstorms, the birds began gathering on the power-line.

At evening he would see the wires like necklaces of blue-and-black glass beads when the swallows gathered. He loved to hear them making excited twittering sounds, he loved to see how they simply fell off the copper wire into space and their perfect curved wings lifted them on the air.

They were going not merely beyond the skyline like the power, they were flying thousands of miles over land and sea and the mountains and forests to countries he had never dreamt of. The birds opened another door for him and he liked them too, very much.

He watched the swallows one morning as they took off from their perch. Suddenly, as if they had a secret signal, a whole stretch of them along a wire would start together. They dropped forward into the air and their blue-and-white wings flicked out. Flying seemed to be the easiest thing in the world. They swooped and flew up, criss-crossing in flight and chirping crazily, so pleased to be awake in the morning.

Then another flight of them winged off, and another. There was standing-room only on those wires. Close to the lofty pylon and the gleaming china ties another flight took off. But one of the swallows stayed behind, quite close to the tie. André watched them fall forward, but it alone did not leave the line. It hung there flapping its wings and he saw it was caught by its leg.

He should have been going to school but he stood watching the swallow, his cap pulled over his white hair and eyes wrinkled against the light. After a minute the swallow stopped flapping and hung there. He wondered how it could have got caught, maybe in the wire binding or at a join. Swallows had short legs and small black claws; he had caught one once in its nest and held it in his hands before it struggled free and was gone in a flash. He thought

43

the bird on the powerline would get free soon, but looking at it there he had a tingling kind of pain in his chest and in one leg as if he too were caught by the foot.

André wanted to rush back and tell his mother, only she would scold him for being late to school. So he climbed on his bike and with one more look up at the helpless bird there against the sky and the steel framework of the tower, he rode off to the bus.

At school he thought once or twice about the swallow, but mostly he forgot about it and that made him feel bad. Anyway, he thought, it would be free by the time he got home.

Coming back from the crossroads he felt anxious, but he did not like to look up until he was quite near. Then he shot one glance at the top of the pylon – the swallow was still there, its wings spread but not moving. It was dead, he guessed, as he stopped and put down one foot. Then he saw it flutter and fold up its wings. He felt awful to think it had hung there all day, trapped.

The boy went in and called his mother and they stood off some distance below the powerline and looked at the bird. The mother shaded her eyes with her hand. It was a pity, she said, but really she was sure it would free itself somehow. Nothing could be done about it.

'Couldn't – ?' he began.

'Couldn't nothing, dear,' she said quite firmly so that he knew she meant business. 'Now stop thinking about it, and tomorrow you'll see.'

His father came home at six and had tea, and afterwards there was a little time to work in his patch of vegetables out at the back. André followed him and he soon got round to the swallow on the powerline.

'I know,' his father said. 'Mama told me.'

'It's still there.'

'Well, – ' his father tilted up his old working-hat and looked at him hard with his sharp blue eyes – 'well, we can't do anything about it, can we, now?'

'No, Papa, but – '

'But what?'

He kicked at a stone and said nothing more. He could see his father was kind of stiff about it; that meant he did not want to hear anything more. They had been talking about it, and maybe – yes, that was it. They were afraid he would try to climb up the pylon.

At supper none of them talked about the swallow, but André felt

44

it all right. He felt as if it was hanging above their heads and his mother and father felt it and they all had a load on them. Going to bed his mother said to him he must not worry himself about the poor bird. 'Not a sparrow falls without our Good Lord knowing.'

'It's not a sparrow, it's a swallow,' he said. 'It's going to hang there all night, by its foot.'

His mother sighed and put out the light. She was worried.

The next day was a Saturday and he did not have to go to school. First thing he looked out and the bird was still there. The other swallows were with it, and when they took off it fluttered and made little thin calls but could not get free.

He would rather have been at school instead of knowing all day that it was hanging up there on the cruel wire. The morning was very long, though he did forget about the swallow quite often. He was building a mud fort under the gum tree, and he had to carry water and dig up the red earth and mix it into a stiff clay.

When he was coming in at midday with his khaki hat flapping round his face he had one more look, and what he saw kept him standing there a long time with his mouth open. Other swallows were fluttering and hovering around the trapped bird, trying to help it. He rushed inside and dragged his mother out by her hand and she stood too, shading her eyes again, and looking up.

'Yes, they're feeding it. Isn't that strange,' she said.

'Ssh! Don't frighten them,' he whispered.

In the afternoon he lay in the grass and twice again he saw the other swallows fluttering round the fastened bird with short quivering strokes of their wings and opening their beaks wide.

André felt choked thinking how they helped it and nobody else would do anything. His parents would not even talk about it.

With his keen eyes he traced the way a climber could get up the tower.

But if you did get up, what then? How could you touch the swallow? Just putting your hand near the wire, wouldn't those millions of volts flame out and jump at you?

The only thing was to get somebody to turn off the power for a minute, then he could whip up the tower like a monkey. At supper that night he suggested it, and his father was as grim and angry as he'd ever seen.

'Listen, son,' his father said. He never said 'son' unless he was really mad about something. 'Listen, I don't want you to get all worked up about that bird. I'll see what can be done. But you leave it alone. Don't get any ideas into your head, and don't go near that accursed pylon.'

'What ideas, Papa?' he asked, trembling inside himself.

'Any ideas at all.'

'The other birds are feeding it, but it may die.'

'Well, I'm sorry; try not to think about it.'

When his mother came to say good night to him he turned his face over into his pillow and would not kiss her. It was something he had never done before and it was because he was angry with them both. They let the swallow swing there in the night and did nothing.

His mother patted his back and ruffled his white hair and said, 'Good night, darling.' But he gritted his teeth and did not answer.

Ages seemed to him to have passed. The bird was still hanging on the lofty powerline, fluttering feebly. He could not bear to look up at it. After breakfast he went out and tried to carry on building his fort under the gum tree. The birds were chattering in the tree above him and in the wattles at the back of the house. Through the corner of his eye he saw a handsome black-and-white bird fly out in swinging loops from the tree and it settled on the powerline some distance from the tower. It was a butcher-bird, a Jackey-hangman, a terrible greedy pirate of a bird.

His heart fell like a stone – he just guessed what it was up to.

The butcher-bird flew off and settled higher up the wire near the pylon.

André rushed up the path and then took a swing from the house to come under the powerline. Stopping, he saw the other birds were making a whirl and flutter round the cannibal. Swallows darted and skimmed and made him duck his head, but he went on sitting there. Then some starlings came screaming out of the gum tree and flew in a menacing bunch at the butcher-bird. They all hated him. He made the mistake of losing his balance and fluttered out into the air and all the birds were round him at once, darting and pecking and screaming.

The butcher-bird pulled off one of his typical tricks – he fell plumb down and when near the ground spread his wings, sailed low over the shrubs, and came up at the house where he settled on the lightning conductor.

André ran towards the house waving his arms and shouting. The bird cocked its head and watched him.

46

His mother came out. 'Darling, what's the matter?'

'That Jackey, he's on the roof. He wanted to kill the swallow.'

'Oh darling!' the mother said softly.

It was Sunday night and he said to his mother, 'It's only the other birds keeping him alive. They were feeding him again today.'

'I saw them.'

'He can't live much longer, Mama. And now the Jackey knows he's there. Why can't Papa get them to switch off the electricity?'

'They wouldn't do it for a bird, darling. Now try and go to sleep.'

Leaving for school, he tried not to look up. But he couldn't help it and there was the swallow spreading and closing its wings. He quickly got on his bike and rode as fast as he could. He could not think of anything but the trapped bird on the powerline.

After school, André did not catch the bus home. Instead, he took a bus the other way, into town. He got out in a busy street and threaded his way down through the factory area.

When he got to the power station he was faced with an enormous high fence of iron staves with spiked tops and a tall steel gate, locked fast.

André peered through the gate and saw some black men off duty, sitting in the sun. He called to them, and a big slow-moving man in brown overalls and a wide leather belt came over to talk.

André explained very carefully what he wanted. If they would switch off the current then he or somebody good at climbing could go up and save the swallow.

The man smiled broadly and clicked his tongue. He shouted something at the others and they laughed. His name, he said, was Gas – Gas Makabeni. He was just a maintenance boy and he couldn't switch off the current. But he unlocked a steel framedoor in the gate and let André in.

'Ask them in there,' he said, grinning. André liked Gas very much. He had in big cloth letters ESCOM done on his back and he was friendly, opening the door like that.

André went with Gas through a high arched entrance and at once he seemed to be surrounded with the vast awesome hum of the power station. It made him feel jumpy. Gas took him to a door and pushed him in.

A white engineer in overalls questioned him and he smiled too. 'Well,' he said. 'Let's see what can be done.'

He led down a long corridor and up a short cut of steel zigzag steps. Another corridor came to an enormous panelled hall with banks of dials and glowing lights and men in long white coats sitting in raised chairs or moving about silently. André's heart was pounding good and fast.

He could hear the humming sound strongly and it seemed to come from everywhere, not so much a sound as a feeling under his feet.

The engineer in overalls handed him over to one of the men at the control panels and he was so nervous by this time he took a long while trying to explain about the swallow. The man had to ask him a lot of questions and he got tongue-tied and could not give clear answers. The man did not smile at all.

He went off and a minute later came and fetched André to a big office. A black-haired man with glasses was sitting at a desk. On both sides of the desk were telephones and panels of push-buttons. There was a carpet on the floor and huge leather easy chairs.

André did not say five words before his lip began trembling and two tears rolled out of his eyes. The man told him, 'Sit down son, and don't be scared.'

Then the man tried to explain. How could they cut off the power when thousands and thousands of machines were running on electricity? The trains would stop, hospitals would go dark in the middle of an operation, the mine skips would suddenly halt eight thousand feet down. He knew André was concerned about the swallow, only things like that just happened and that was life.

'Life?' André said, thinking it more like death.

The big man smiled. He took down André's name and address, and he said, 'You've done your best, André. I'm sorry I can't promise you anything.'

Downstairs again, Gas Makabeni let him out at the gate. 'Are they switching off the power?' Gas asked.

'No.'

'Mayi babo!' Gas shook his head and clicked. But he did not smile this time. He could see the boy was very unhappy.

André got home hours late and his mother was frantic. He lied to her too, saying he had been detained after school. He kept his eyes away from the powerline and did not have the stomach to look for the swallow. He felt so bad about it because they were all letting it die. Except for the other swallows that brought it food, it would be dead already.

And that was life, the man said....

It must have been the middle of the night when he woke up. His mother was in the room in her kimono and the light was on. 'There's a man come to see you,' she said. 'Did you ask anyone to come here?'

'No, Mama,' he said, dazed.

'Get up and come.' She sounded cross and he was scared stiff. He went out on the stoep and there he saw his father in his pyjamas and the back of a big man in brown overalls with ESCOM on them: a black man. It was Gas Makabeni!

'Gas!' he shouted. 'Are they going to do it?'

'They're doing it,' Gas said.

A linesman and a truckdriver came up the steps on the stoep. The linesman explained to André's father a maintenance switchdown had been ordered at minimum-load hour. He wanted to be shown where the bird was. André glanced, frightened, at his father who nodded and said, 'Show him.'

He went in the maintenance truck with the man and the driver and Gas. It took them only five minutes to get the truck in position under the tower. The maintenance man checked the time and they began running up the extension ladder. Gas hooked a chain in his broad belt and pulled on his flashlight helmet. He swung out on the ladder and began running up it as if he had no weight at all. Up level with the pylon insulators, his flashlight picked out the swallow hanging on the dead wire. He leaned over and carefully worked the bird's tiny claw loose from the wire binding and then he put the swallow in the breastpocket of his overalls.

In a minute he was down again and he took the bird out and handed it to the boy. André could see even in the light of the flashlamp that the swallow had faint grey fringes round the edges of its shining blue-black feathers and that meant it was a young bird. This was its first year. He was almost speechless, holding the swallow in his hands and feeling its slight quiver.

'Thanks,' he said. 'Thanks, Gas. Thanks, mister.'

His father took the swallow from him at the house and went off to find a box to keep it out of reach of the cats.

'Off you go to bed now,' the mother said. 'You've had quite enough excitement for one day.'

The swallow drank thirstily but would not eat anything they could think of, so the parents thought it best to let it go as soon as it would fly. André took the box to his fort near the gum tree looking out towards the koppie and the powerline. He held the swallow in his cupped hands and it lay there quiet with the tips of its wings crossed. Then it suddenly took two little jumps with its tiny claws and spread its slender wings. Frantically its wings beat the air and it seemed to be dropping to the ground.

Then it skimmed forward only a foot above the grass and he remembered long afterwards how, when it really took wing and began to gain height, it gave a little shiver of happiness as if it knew it was free.

Starting points

1. *Look through the story again and jot down all the examples you can find of different kinds of power, including the powers that grown-ups have. Use your notes to help you talk in a group about the powers each person in the story possesses (including André).*

2. *Talk about a situation in which you felt powerless and then compare your feelings with how André felt as he watched the trapped swallow. Then use your situation as the starting point for a story of your own.*

3. *Re-tell the events of the story from the point of view of either André's mother or his father.*

4. *Re-read the episode at the power station and re-write it as a script for a radio play. Try out your script with a small group of people taking the parts and, if possible, record it.*
   Or:
   In pairs, dramatize the scene between André and the chief engineer at the power station.

THE KISS

Walter Macken

IT was a most beautiful morning. The white clouds, above this part of the Irish coast, seemed playful and benign. The waters of the river went over the weir like a flow of silk and emptied placidly, a short distance farther on, into the sea. The flowers on the far bank of the river were white and purple. Many small, brightly coloured pleasure boats were tied up along the near bank, waiting for the tourists to get out of their beds.

The boy paid not the least attention to those real boats. Standing on a ramp leading into the river, he sailed his own boat. It was a short piece of rough timber, the front of which he had shaped very crudely into a sort of bow. He had put a nail in the bow, and tied a long string to it. He would push his boat out into the water, and it would wobble its way towards where there was a slight pull from the current, and as it set off towards the weir he would pull the string and the boat would turn reluctantly, half drowned, back towards him. He was about nine years old, with brown, curly hair. He wore a shirt, short trousers, and sandals; the sandals were wet, and one of them had a broken strap.

Sometimes his boat was a great battleship. He would purse his lips and make big-gun sounds. Sometimes it was an ocean liner, tall and majestic, and he would make a deep siren sound from his chest. It was also a fussy tug, a river boat. It was anything he wanted it to be, and he thought it was wonderful.

Then this girl came along by the riverside. She was six or so. She had fair hair and a short dress that showed her well-browned limbs, which were in the pudgy stage. She had blue eyes and fat wrists, and she was still inclined to bite one finger. She was pulling a wooden horse by a string over the uneven ground. It was on wobbly wheels, this horse, and was painted white, with red trimmings. When it toppled, she would stop and put it upright and go on again. She came to the ramp and stood there and watched the boy playing with the boat. 'Hello, Jimmy,' she said.

Jimmy gave her one glance over his shoulder. He wished her to go away. She knew this, but it didn't embarrass her. She just squatted down and watched him – boat in, boat out. Like Jimmy, she thought it was a beautiful boat.

'Nice boat,' she said.

He raised one eyebrow to look at her. He didn't smile, but he was pleased that she knew a beautiful thing when she saw it. 'Huh,' he said.

'Could you carry my horse across the river?' she asked. She asked that as if it were an impossible thing.

Jimmy considered it. He knew she thought that he couldn't possibly do such a thing, so he said, with scorn, 'Of course! Bring the horse down to the dock.'

She rose from her squatting, and very carefully pulled the horse to the edge of the ramp. She wished to show him that she could handle a horse well. As the boat was then in midstream, he had to turn it with finesse.

He used the string gently, so that when the boat turned it didn't even go under the water. Like a master mariner, he brought it safely to port.

'You will have to back the horse on to the ship,' he said. 'Careful. You might swamp the boat and there is no insurance on her.'

'I'll be careful,' she said. She put her small red tongue between her teeth and held it there as she started backing the horse on board. The horse would take up a lot of room – nearly the whole width and length of the boat. She was conscious of a critical eye watching her and when finally the horse stood on the boat she clapped her hands and said, 'Now!'

'That was easy,' the boy said. 'Now it is hard.'

The weight of the horse was almost submerging the vessel, so he was very cautious. He gently eased the boat and its burden out into the water with his little finger, and as the flow of the stream caught the boat he loosed the guiding string with extreme care. They held their breath. The boat went out the full length of the string. It wobbled a bit. The girl bit at her finger.

'Crossing the rapids is the worst part,' the boy said as he delicately began turning the boat and its burden around. Slowly it came around, little by little, and then, after a few terrible moments of anxiety, it started to come back to them. They were standing by, tense, as he brought it in. Finally, it scraped against the ramp. He bent down, pulled the horse on to the ramp, and then, standing up, he said, 'Now you will have to pay!'

To his astonishment, the little girl clapped her hands and said, 'Oh, Jimmy!' and stood on her toes and kissed him.

It was this sight the priest saw as he glanced up from his breviary. He thought it was a most wonderful sight. He was pleased with the morning, the summer sun, the flowers, and the green leaves. The psalms of his office were in praise of the material works of God, and this sight to him was the climax of the morning. He was pleased he had come to the riverside.

Jimmy was about to wipe his mouth with the back of his hand where she had kissed him, when this tall figure of a priest dressed in black loomed over them. He was smiling. 'Oh, this won't do,' the priest said. 'I saw you kissing Jimmy, Cecily. Now you will have to be married. You know that.' He was marking his place in the breviary with the index finger of his right hand. He put his hand on Jimmy's head and his free hand on Cecily's head. 'Now,' he said, laughing, 'you are married.'

He was very pleased with his joke. He looked at their innocence and smiled, and then walked on, chuckling. It was a little time before he could erase the picture they made and get on with his office.

Jimmy was glaring at the little girl. His fists were clenched. 'Now see what you have done,' he said.

'What?' she asked.

'Everything! Everything!' he shouted. 'You have ruined every-thing!'

He saw her face starting to crumble. He bent down, took his boat, string and all, and fired it out into the river. He watched it as it went under the water and then popped up again and settled. It was near the weir. It went around and around and then it was gone. He felt sad. He felt it was the total end of a way of life.

'Come on!' he said roughly to the girl. She was biting her finger now. He snatched this hand from her mouth and took it in his own. Her finger was wet. He bent over and took the horse in his other hand. 'Come on!' he said again, and walked off with her. She had to run to keep up with him.

He walked her from the riverside, up one street and into another street. He knew her house well. It was only a few doors from his own. The door of her house was open to the sun. The red tiles of the front step were polished. 'Go in, now,' he said, 'and don't stir out again.' She went in and stood, looking back at him. There were tears in her eyes. 'And don't be biting your finger. You are not a cannibal,' he added, and left her. She watched him go. Then she came out and sat on the step. She reached for her horse he had set down there, and cuddled it in her arms. She was bewildered.

Jimmy wondered where he would go first. Somewhere away from home he would have to go. It wouldn't do near home. Everyone left home when a thing like this happened. He thought of places he had been with his father. They might know him, those shopkeepers. He headed for the shops. It was quite a walk. He had to stop now and again to pull the sandal with the broken strap up on his heel. Down into town and along the main street and across the bridge and down another few streets. He saw this shop where his father often took him. He went in. He liked the smell of it. Raisins and spices and fruit and at the back a closed-off place where his father would drink a glass of stout and Jimmy would have fizzy lemonade and a biscuit with currants in it; he would pull out the currants and eat them before he threw away the biscuit.

'Mr Moran,' he said to the shopkeeper.

Moran had to bend over the counter to see where the voice came from. 'Ah, hello, Jimmy,' he said. 'Do you want a pint?'

'No, sir,' said Jimmy. 'I want a job.'

'Oh! Ah!' exclaimed Mr Moran and roared with laughter. 'Hey, Dominic,' he called to a man in a white apron. 'Here's a fella after your job.'

'Don't be laughing, Mr Moran,' said Jimmy, desperately.

'What do you want me to do?' Moran asked. 'Now, look at the size of you. You couldn't reach the bottom shelf. God – you're a comic, Jimmy. Come back when you've grown four feet.'

But Jimmy was gone. His face was red. He was digging his nails into his palms. Why wouldn't they understand? They shouldn't laugh.

The man in the hotel laughed. He called a lot of people to look at Jimmy and tell them what Jimmy had said. The man in the fun palace laughed. His laughter and the laughter of his clients followed Jimmy as he ran towards the sea.

There he sat on the rocks. The tide was coming in, and he flung round stones at the sea. He felt really desperate. He understood, now, all the hardships of being grown up.

Jimmy's father's heart didn't return to its proper position until he saw the lonely figure on the stony beach. He left his bicycle on the promenade and walked down to him. He's alive, he was thinking. Imagine, he's alive! When Jimmy hadn't come home for lunch, he had begun searching for him; that was two hours ago. He had been thinking of getting the river dragged, thinking of small bodies caught at the weir.

'Hello, Jimmy,' he said, sitting beside him. Jimmy looked at him. His father's face was serious. This pleased Jimmy. 'You didn't come home for your grub,' his father said. 'I was looking all over the place for you.' He had heard about Jimmy's looking for a job. 'Did something happen?'

'Yes,' said Jimmy. 'It was that silly Cecily. We're married.'

'Oh,' said his father. But he didn't laugh. Jimmy noticed that and put his hand on his father's knee, and after a pause, Jimmy's father put his own hand on the small one. 'Married?' he said. 'I see.'

Jimmy told him about the priest. 'So I had to go looking for a job,' he said, 'and go away from home.'

'I see,' said his father. 'I see.' But, again, he didn't laugh. 'That's serious, right enough. It's a tough life.'

'What am I going to do now?' Jimmy asked. 'Nobody wants a boy to work for them. I'm too small.'

'The best thing we can do is to go and see that priest,' said Jimmy's father.

'Will that do any good?' Jimmy asked.

'You never know,' said his father. 'Come on.'

He put him on the bar of the bicycle, and they went into town and over to the house of the priest. I hope, Jimmy's father was thinking, that he will understand the feelings of a small boy.

'Will he be able to do anything?' Jimmy asked, as they stood at the front door.

'They have great power,' said Jimmy's father, ringing the bell.

The priest's housekeeper showed them into a room lined with books. Jimmy was very nervous. The priest came in. He smiled when he saw Jimmy. 'Ah, Jimmy,' he said. 'Hello, Joe, what ails you?'

'I believe,' Joe said slowly, 'that you married my son to Cecily this morning.' Don't laugh now, Father, he thought, because you are the one that started it.

Jimmy was watching the priest slowly. The priest didn't laugh. He nodded, and sat down in a leather-covered chair. Joining his fingers together to cover his mouth, he said 'Ah!'

'So Jimmy did the right thing,' said his father. 'He went looking everywhere for a job to support Cecily.'

'Hmm,' said the priest. 'Cecily would be an expensive wife.'

'You should see her eating ice cream,' said Jimmy.

'I see,' said the priest. 'Tell me, did you go into her house at all since you were married?'

'I did not,' said Jimmy.

'You mean you didn't go into her house and have a meal or anything?'

'I did not,' said Jimmy scornfully.

'Ah, then it's all off,' said the priest.

'It is?' said Jimmy.

'Certainly,' said the priest. 'If you don't go and live in the same house as Cecily, it's all off.'

'I'll never go near her again as long as I live,' said Jimmy.

'That's a pity,' said the priest. 'I thought you were a nice couple.'

'She's a silly girl,' said Jimmy.

'Incompatibility,' said the priest. 'So you are as free as a bird again, Jimmy.'

'I'm glad! I'm glad! I'm glad!' said Jimmy.

The priest and his father wondered at the fervent way he spoke.

'Thank you, Father,' said Joe. 'You are very kind.'

'No,' said the priest. 'I'm very silly.' Jimmy was running into the hall towards the door. 'They were such a pretty picture. I meant no harm. That silly joke, and it gives a boy many hours of worry. Who would think it?'

He watched father and son go out the door. Jimmy was a different boy from the one who had stood in the room with the books. He was chattering now, joggling about on the bar of the bicycle. Joe waved at the priest, and then they were gone.

Joe thought how relieved his wife would be to see Jimmy. He thought of the change that had come over his son. He wondered if he would remember this when he was grown up. He himself would never forget it. He wondered if, somehow, it was his fault. He wondered if he was responsible for something buried deep in the mind of his son that had caused this simple joke of the priest to bring such terror. He wondered if his son would ever understand what had happened.

Jimmy was honking from his chest as if he were the horn of a motorcar.

Starting points

1. Look through the story again and jot down those occasions when confusions and misinterpretations happen. Talk about these and what causes them.

2. 'No,' said the priest. 'I'm very silly.' Trace the part played by the priest in the story. Do you agree with his view of himself? Re-tell the events of the story from the priest's point of view.

3. Talk with another person about a time when you felt an adult did not understand you or about an occasion when a joke turned out badly. Make the episode into a story of your own and ask your partner to read it and suggest improvements.

4. In the story we learn that Jimmy's father had 'heard about Jimmy's looking for a job'. Working with a partner, prepare a drama script of the conversation that might have taken place between Jimmy's father and Mr Moran. Try out your script together.

THE
PEPPER-TREE

Dal Stivens

MY father often spoke about the pepper-tree when we were kids, and it was clear it meant a lot to him. It stood for something – like the Rolls Royce he was always going to buy. It wasn't what he said about the pepper-tree – my father had no great gift for words – but how he said it that counted. When he spoke of the pepper-tree at Tullama where he had been brought up you saw it clearly; a monster of a tree with long shawls of olive-green leaves in a big generous country-town backyard. 'A decent backyard – none of your city pocket-handkerchief lots,' my father said. There were berries on the tree that turned from green to pink with waxlike covers which you could unpick and get the sticky smell of them all over your fingers. In this spanking tree there was always, too, a noisy traffic of sparrows and starlings fluttering and hopping from branch to branch.

When we lived at Newtown, Sydney, I used to look for pepper-trees when my father took me for a walk on Sunday afternoons. 'Look, there's a pepper-tree,' I'd say to him when I saw one with its herring-bone leaves.

'By golly, boy, that's only a little runt of a tree,' my old man would say. 'They don't do so well in the city. Too much smoke, by golly. You ought to see them out west where I come from.'

My father was a tall, thin man with melancholy brown eyes and the soul of a poet. It was the poet in him that wanted to own a Rolls Royce one day.

'First our own house and then some day, when my ship comes home, I'll buy a Rolls Royce,' he'd say.

Some of his friends thought my old man was a little crazy to have such an ambition.

'What would you do with one of those flash cars, Peter?' they'd tease him. 'Go and live among the swells?'

My father would stroke his long brown moustache, which had only a few bits of white in it, and try to explain, but he couldn't make them understand. He couldn't even get his ideas across to my mother. Only now do I think I understand what a Rolls Royce meant to him.

'I don't want to swank it, as you put it, Emily,' he'd say to my mother. 'No, by golly. I want to own a Rolls Royce because it is the most perfect piece of machinery made in this world. Why, a Rolls Royce – '

And then he'd stop and you could feel him groping for the right words to describe what he felt, and then go on blunderingly with the caress of a lover in his voice, talking about how beautiful the engine was....

'What would a garage mechanic do with a Rolls Royce, I ask you!' my mother would say. 'I'd feel silly sitting up in it.'

At such times my mother would give the wood stove in the kitchen a good shove with the poker, or swish her broom vigorously. My mother was a small plump woman with brown hair which she wore drawn tight back from her forehead.

Like the pepper-tree, the Rolls Royce symbolized something for my father. He had been born in Tullama in the mallee. His father was a bricklayer and wanted his son to follow him. But my father had had his mind set on becoming an engineer. When he was eighteen he had left Tullama and come to the city and got himself apprenticed to a mechanical engineer. He went to technical classes in the evening. After two years his eyes had given out on him.

'If I had had some money things might have been different, by golly,' my father told me once. 'I could have gone to the university and learnt things properly. I could have become a civil engineer. I didn't give my eyes a fair go – I went to classes five nights a week and studied after I came home.'

After his eyes went, my father had to take unskilled jobs but always near machinery. 'I like tinkering but I had no proper schooling,' he said once.

He knew a lot and in spite of his eyes he could only have learnt most of it from books. He knew all about rocks and how they were formed. He could talk for hours, if you got him started, about fossils and the story of evolution. My mother didn't like to hear him talking about such things because she thought such talk was irreligious. Looking back now I'd say that in spite of his lack of orthodox schooling my father was a learned man. He taught me more than all the teachers I ever had at high school. He was a keen naturalist, too.

Just before the depression came when we were living at Newtown, my father had paid one hundred pounds off the house. He was forty-seven years old then. I was twelve.

'By golly, we'll own the house before we know where we are,' he said.

'Will we?' said my mother. 'At a pound a week we have twelve years to go – unless we win Tatts.'

'You never know what may turn up,' said my old man cheerfully.

'I have a good idea what with people losing their jobs every day.'

'I haven't lost mine,' my father said, 'and what's more, if I do, I have a way of making some money.'

'I suppose it's another of your inventions, Peter? What is it this time, I ask you?'

'Never you mind,' said my father. But he said it gently.

One of my mother's complaints was that my father was always losing money on the things he tried to invent. Another was that he was always filling the backyard up with junk.

'What can you do with these pocket-handkerchief lots?' my father would say. 'Now, when I was a nipper at Tullama we had a decent backyard – why it was immense – it was as big – '

He'd stop there not being able to get the right word.

Auction sales, according to my mother, were one of my father's weaknesses. He could never resist anything if it looked cheap, even if he had no use for it, she'd say. Soon after my old man had told my mother he had something in mind to make some money, he went away one Sunday morning. He came back about lunch-time in a motor lorry. On the back of the Ford was a two-stroke kerosene engine. I came running out.

'I've bought it, Joe, by golly,' he told me.

He had, too. Both engine and lorry.

'Dirt cheap. Forty quid the lot,' he said. 'Ten quid down, boy, and ten bob a week.'

My mother cut up when she heard.

'Wasting money when it could have gone into the house, Peter.'

'This'll pay the house off in no time, by golly,' my father said. 'And buy a lot of other things, too.'

60

I knew by the way he looked up and over my mother's head he was thinking of the Rolls Royce which to him was like a fine poem or a great symphony of Beethoven.

All that day he was very excited, walking round the engine, standing back to admire it, and then peering closely at it. He started it running and stopped it continually all the afternoon. Every night when he came home from the garage during the next week, he'd go first thing and look at the engine. He had some plan in his mind but wouldn't say what it was at first.

'Wait and see, Joe,' he'd said. 'You'll see all right.'

He didn't let me into his secret for over a week, although I knew he was bursting to tell someone. In the end, he drew me aside mysteriously in the kitchen one night, when my mother was in the bedroom, and whispered, 'It's an invention for cleaning out underground wells, boy.'

'For cleaning out wells?'

'Underground wells.'

He listened to hear if my mother was coming back.

'I'm rigging a light out there tonight, boy,' he whispered. 'Come out later and I'll show you.'

My father's idea, he explained later, was to clean underground wells in country towns by suction. You pushed a stiff brush on the end of the pipe down the sides and along the bottom of underground wells. The pipe sucked up the silt and you didn't lose much water from the well.

'Every country town has half a dozen underground wells, boy,' he said. 'The banks and one or two of the wealthier blokes in the town. Just like it was in Tullama. There's money in it because you can clean the well out without losing too much water. It's a gold-mine.'

It sounded good to me.

'When do you start?' I asked.

'Soon, by golly,' he said. 'The job at the garage won't spin out much longer.'

He was right about that, but until the day she died my mother always had a sneaking idea that the old man had helped to give himself the sack. It was early in 1930 when the old man set out in the lorry, heading out west.

'You've got to go to the low-rainfall districts,' he said.

'Like Tullama?' I said.

'Yes, like Tullama, by golly.'

I started thinking of the pepper-tree then.

'Will you go to Tullama and see the pepper-tree?'

My father stroked his long straggling moustache. Into his eyes came that look like when he was thinking or talking about the Rolls. He didn't answer me for a bit.

'By golly, yes boy, if I go there.'

Soon after this he started off. Every week brought a letter from him. He did well too. He was heading almost due west from Sydney and I followed the towns he spoke of in my school atlas. It took him nearly a day on a well, so in the larger towns he might stay over a week, in the smaller a day or a day and a half.

After he had been away for two months he still had a good few wells to go before he reached Tullama. You could see that he was headed that way.

'Him and that silly pepper-tree!' said my mother, but she didn't say it angrily. My father was sending her as much money as he used to bring home when he worked at the garage.

But in spite of what my mother said about the pepper-tree she became a bit keen as my father got only two weeks off Tullama. She made a small pin-flag for me to stick on the map. About this time a change came in the old man's letters home. At first they had been elated, but now they were quieter. He didn't boast so much about the money he was making, or say anything about the Rolls. Perhaps excitement was making him quieter as he got nearer to the pepper-tree, I thought.

'I know what it is,' my mother said. 'He's not getting his proper meals. He's too old to be gallivanting off on his own. I bet he's not cooking proper meals for himself. And without a decent bed to sleep in – only the back of that lorry.'

I thought the day would never come, but soon enough my dad had only one town to do before he would reach Tullama. His letters usually arrived on a Tuesday – he wrote home on the Sundays – but round this time I watched for the mail every day and was late for school three mornings running. When a letter did come I grabbed it from the postman's hand and hurried inside with it, reading the postmark on the run. It was from Tullama.

'All right, all right, don't rush me, Joe,' my mother said. 'You and your pepper-tree.'

I read over her elbow. There was only one page. There was nothing about the pepper-tree. Dad was well and making money, but he was thinking of returning soon. Only a few lines.

I couldn't understand it.

On the next Tuesday there was no letter. Nor on the Wednesday. On the Thursday my father came home. He turned up at breakfast-time. He gave us a surprise walking in like that. He said that he had sold the truck and engine and come home by train. He looked tired and shamefaced and somehow a lot older. I saw a lot more white in his moustache.

'The engine was no good,' he said. 'It kept breaking down. It cost me nearly all I earned and it was hungry on petrol. I had to sell it to pay back what I borrowed and get my fare home.'

'Oh, Peter,' my mother said, putting her arms round him. 'You poor darling. I knew something was wrong.'

'Mother reckoned it was the food,' I said. 'She reckoned you weren't getting your proper meals.'

'I'll make you a cup of tea, Peter,' my mother said, bustling over to the stove and pushing another piece of wood into it. 'Then I'll get you some breakfast.'

'By golly, that sounds a bit of all right,' my father said then. This was the first time since he had walked in that he had sounded like his old self.

My mother hurried about the kitchen and my father talked a bit more. 'I thought I was going to do well at first,' he said. 'But the engine was too old. It was always spare parts. It ate up all I earned.'

He talked on about the trip. I had got over my surprise at seeing him walk in and now wanted to know all about the pepper-tree.

'Did you see the pepper-tree, dad?'

'Yes, I saw it all right.'

I stood directly in front of him as he sat at the table, but he was not looking at me but at something far away. He didn't answer for what seemed a long time.

'It was a little runt of a tree, boy – and a little backyard.'

He wouldn't say any more than that and he never spoke of the pepper-tree – or the Rolls – again.

Starting points

1. *Make notes about the kind of person Peter, the boy's father, is. Take your evidence from what he says and what he does. Use your notes to talk together in a group about how he changes and why.*

2. *Talk about an occasion when you looked forward eagerly to some event, but were very disappointed by the reality. Write your story, making clear as you go exactly how you felt.*

3. *Working in pairs, prepare a programme for local radio about the journey west made by Peter. One person is the interviewer; the other is Peter. Try out your interview and, if you have time, record it.*

4. *With another person, talk about why dreams for the future and memories of the past are important to Peter. Are they also important to you? Which early memories do you value? What dreams for the future do you have and how realistic are they?*

THE
RAIN HORSE

Ted Hughes

AS the young man came over the hill the first thin blowing of rain met him. He turned his coat-collar up and stood on top of the shelving rabbit-riddled hedgebank, looking down into the valley.

For twelve years, whenever he had recalled this scene, he had imagined it as it looked from here. Now the valley lay sunken in front of him, utterly deserted, shallow, bare fields, black and sodden as the bed of an ancient lake after weeks of rain.

Twelve years had changed him. This land no longer recognised him, and he looked back at it coldly, as at a finally visited home-country, known only through the stories of a grandfather; felt nothing but the dullness of feeling nothing. Boredom. Then, suddenly, impatience, with a whole exasperated swarm of little anxieties about his shoes and the spitting rain and his new suit and that sky and the two-mile trudge through the mud back to the road.

A wave of anger went over him: anger against himself for blundering into this mud-trap and anger against the land that made him feel so outcast, so old and stiff and stupid. He wanted nothing but to get away from it as quickly as possible. But as he turned, something moved in his eye-corner. All his senses startled alert. He stopped.

Over to his right a thin, black horse was running across the ploughland towards the hill, its head down, neck stretched out. It seemed to be running on its toes like a cat, like a dog up to no good.

From the high point on which he stood the hill dipped slightly and rose to another crested point fringed with the tops of trees, three hundred yards to his right. As he watched it, the horse ran up to that crest, showed against the sky – for a moment like a nightmarish leopard – and disappeared over the other side.

For several seconds he stared at the skyline, stunned by the unpleasantly strange impression the horse had made on him. Then the plastering beat of icy rain on his bare skull brought him to himself. The distance had vanished in a wall of grey. All around him the fields were jumping and streaming.

Holding his collar close and tucking his chin down into it he ran back over the hilltop, his feet sucking and splashing, at every stride plunging to the ankle.

This hill was shaped like a wave, a gently rounded back lifting out of the valley to a sharply crested, almost concave front hanging over the river meadows towards the town. Down this front, from the crest, hung two small woods separated by a fallow field.

He ran along the top of the first wood and finding no shelter but the thin, leafless thorns of the hedge, dipped below the crest out of the wind and jogged along through thick grass to the wood of oaks. In blinding rain he lunged through the barricade of brambles at the wood's edge. The little crippled trees were small choice in the way of shelter, but at a sudden fierce thickening of the rain he took one at random and crouched down under the leaning trunk.

Still panting from his run, drawing his knees up tightly, he watched the bleak lines of rain, grey as hail, slanting through the boughs into the clumps of bracken and bramble. He felt hidden and safe. The sound of the rain as it rushed and lulled in the wood seemed to seal him in. Soon the chilly sheet lead of his suit became a tight, warm mould, and gradually he sank into a state of comfort that was all but trance, though the rain beat steadily on his exposed shoulders and trickled down the oak trunk on to his neck.

All around him the boughs angled down, glistening, black as iron. From their tips and elbows the drops hurried steadily, and the channels of the bark pulsed and gleamed.

He wanted this rain to go on for ever. Whenever it seemed to be drawing off he listened anxiously until it closed in again. As long as it lasted he was suspended from life and time. He didn't want to return to his sodden shoes and his possibly ruined suit and the walk back over that land of mud.

All at once he shivered. He hugged his knees to squeeze out the cold and found himself thinking of the horse.

He tried to dismiss the thought. Horses wander about the countryside often enough. To clear his mind, he twisted around and looked up the wood between the tree stems, to his left.

At the wood top, with the silvered grey light coming in behind it, the black horse was standing under the oaks, its head high and alert, its ears pricked, watching him.

He turned back. His scalp went icy and he shivered.

This was absurd. He took control of himself and turned back deliberately, determined not to give the horse one more thought. If it wanted to share the wood with him, let it. If it wanted to stare at him, let it. He was nestling firmly into these resolutions when the ground shook and he heard the crash of a heavy body coming down the wood. Like lightning his legs bounded him upright and about face. The horse was almost on top of him, its head stretching forward, ears flattened and lips lifted back from the long yellow teeth. He got one snapshot glimpse of the red-veined eyeball as he flung himself backwards around the tree. Then he was away up the slope, whipped by oak twigs as he leapt the branches and brushwood, twisting between the close trees till he tripped and sprawled. As he fell the warning flashed through his head that he must at all costs keep his suit out of the leaf-mould, but a more urgent instinct was already rolling him violently sideways. He spun around, sat up, and looked back, ready to scramble off in a flash to one side. He was panting from the sudden excitement and effort. The horse had disappeared. The wood was empty except for the drumming, slant grey rain, dancing the bracken and glittering from the branches.

He got up, furious. Knocking the dirt and leaves from his suit as well as he could, he looked around for a weapon. The horse was evidently mad, or maybe it was just spiteful. Rain sometimes puts creatures into queer states. Whatever it was, he was going to get away from the wood as quickly as possible, rain or no rain.

As he went, he broke a yard length of wrist-thick dead branch from one of the oaks, but immediately threw it aside and wiped the slime of rotten wet bark from his hands with his soaked handkerchief. Already he was thinking it incredible that the horse could have meant to attack him.

The wood rose to a steep bank topped by a hawthorn hedge that ran along the whole ridge of the hill. He was pulling himself up to a thin place in the hedge by the bare stem of one of the hawthorns when he ducked and shrank down again. The swelling gradient of fields lay in front of him, smoking in the slowly crossing rain. Out in the middle of the first field, tall as a statue, and a ghostly silver in the undercloud light, stood the horse, watching the wood.

He lowered his head slowly, slithered back down the bank and crouched. An awful feeling of helplessness came over him. He felt certain the horse had been looking straight at him. Waiting for him? Was it clairvoyant? Maybe a mad animal can be clairvoyant. At the same time he was ashamed to find himself acting so inanely, ducking and creeping about in this way just to keep out of sight of a horse. He tried to imagine how anybody in their senses would just walk off home. This cooled him a little, and he retreated farther down the wood. He would go back the way he had come, along under the hill crest, without any more nonsense.

At the woodside he paused, close against a tree. The success of this last manoeuvre was restoring his confidence, but he didn't want to venture out into the open field without making sure that the horse was just where he had left it. He crept up again among the trees to the crest and peeped through the hedge.

The grey field and the whole slope were empty. He searched the distance. The horse was quite likely to have forgotten him altogether and wandered off. Then he raised himself and leaned out to see if it had come in close to the hedge. Before he was aware of anything the ground shook. He twisted around wildly to see how he had been caught. The black shape was above him, right across the light. Its whinnying snort and the spattering whack of its hooves seemed to be actually inside his head as he fell backwards down the bank, and leapt again like a madman, dodging among the oaks, imagining how the buffet would come and how he would be knocked headlong. Half-way down the wood the oaks gave way to bracken and old roots and stony rabbit diggings. He was well out into the middle of this before he realised that he was running alone.

Gasping for breath now and cursing mechanically, without a thought for his suit he sat down on the ground to rest his shaking legs, letting the rain plaster the hair down over his forehead and watching the dense flashing lines disappear abruptly into the soil all around him as if he were watching through thick plate glass.

However, this last attack had cleared up one thing. He need no longer act like a fool out of mere uncertainty as to whether the horse was simply being playful or not. It was definitely after him. He picked up two stones about the size of goose eggs and set off toward the bottom of the wood, striding carelessly.

Now he noticed that the sky had grown much darker. The rain was heavier every second, pressing down as if the earth had to be flooded before nightfall. The oaks ahead blurred and the ground drummed. He began to run. And as he ran he heard a deeper sound running with him. He whirled around. The horse was in the middle of the clearing. It might have been running to get out of the terrific rain except that it was coming straight for him, scattering clay and stones, with an immensely supple and powerful motion. He let out a tearing roar and threw the stone in his right hand. The result was instantaneous. Whether at the roar or the stone the horse reared as if against a wall and shied to the left. As it dropped back on its forefeet he flung his second stone, at ten yards' range, and saw a bright mud blotch suddenly appear on the glistening black flank. The horse surged down the wood, splashing the earth like water, tossing its long tail as it plunged out of sight among the hawthorns.

He looked around for stones. The encounter had set the blood beating in his head and given him a savage energy. He could have killed the horse at that moment. That this brute should pick him and play with him in this malevolent fashion was more than he could bear. Whoever owned it, he thought, deserved to have its neck broken for letting the dangerous thing loose.

He came out at the woodside, in open battle now, still searching for the right stones. There were plenty here, piled and scattered where they had been ploughed out of the field. He selected two, then straightened and saw the horse twenty yards off in the middle of the steep field, watching him calmly. They looked at each other.

'Out of it!' he shouted, brandishing his arm. 'Out of it! Go on!' The horse twitched its pricked ears. With all his force he threw. The stone soared and landed beyond with a soft thud. He re-armed and threw again. For several minutes he kept up his bombardment without a single hit, working himself into a despair and throwing more and more wildly, till his arm began to ache with the unaccustomed exercise. Throughout the performance the horse watched him fixedly. Finally he had to stop and ease his shoulder muscles. As if the horse had been waiting for just this, it dipped its head twice and came at him.

He snatched up two stones and roaring with all his strength flung the one in his right hand. He was astonished at the crack of the impact. It was as if he had struck a tile – and the horse actually stumbled. With another roar he jumped forward and hurled his other stone. His aim seemed to be under superior guidance. The stone struck and rebounded straight up into the air, spinning fiercely, as the horse swirled away and went careering down towards the far bottom corner of the field, at first with great, swinging leaps, then at a canter, leaving deep churned holes in the soil.

It turned up the far side of the field, climbing till it was level with him. He felt a little surprise of pity to see it shake its head, and once it paused to lower its head and paw over its ear with its forehoof as a cat does.

'You stay there!' he shouted. 'Keep your distance and you'll not get hurt.'

And indeed the horse did stop at that moment, almost obediently. It watched him as he climbed up to the crest.

The rain swept into his face and he realised that he was freezing, as if his very flesh were sodden. The farm seemed miles away over the dreary fields. Without another glance at the horse – he felt too exhausted to care now what it did – he loaded the crook of his left arm with stones and plunged out on to the waste of mud.

He was half-way to the first hedge before the horse appeared silhouetted against the sky at the corner of the wood, head high and attentive, watching his laborious retreat over the three fields.

The ankle-deep clay dragged at him. He fought to keep his breathing even, two strides in, two strides out, the air ripping his lungs. In the middle of the last field he stopped and looked around. The horse, tiny on the skyline, had not moved.

At the corner of the field he unlocked his clasped arms and dumped the stones by the gatepost, then leaned on the gate. The farm was in front of him. Making an effort, he heaved his weight over the gate-top. He leaned again, looking up at the hill.

Rain was dissolving land and sky together like a wet water-colour as the afternoon darkened. He concentrated, raising his head, searching the skyline from end to end. The horse had vanished. The hill looked lifeless and desolate, an island lifting out of the sea, awash with every tide.

Starting points

1. *Talk about a time when you were scared by something quite ordinary. Write about an ordinary person or animal that, in your story, behaves in a frightening way.*

2. *Working in pairs, organize an interview for radio with the person in the story. The radio interviewer should encourage a description of how the man felt in the story and how he feels now that the events of the story are behind him.*

3. *Look over the events in the story and trace how the man's feelings about the horse change and develop.*

4. *Working in twos, think up a situation in which one person hunts another and then is hunted or attacked in turn. If you have enough space try out your scene and then compare it with 'The Rain Horse'.*

A FRIEND

Dorothy Whipple

I was aware, very early, of the power of grown-up people. With a word they could destroy your leaping hopes or deprive you of something you cherished with passion. They seemed not only tyrannical, but incalculable; you could never tell beforehand when or why they were going to approve or disapprove.

In the matter of friends, for instance, they never seemed to like the ones you liked yourself. Their *choice* of friends for us was lamentable. They would invite some smug boy or neat little girl to tea, make a fuss over them because we did not, and when they had gone, exclaim: 'Now why can't you behave like that?' They judged children by their manners at table, which was almost the only place they saw them. If children had good manners they approved of them. With us, it was the other way round. We found that those who were the most fun to play with made the worst show at meals.

I suppose, however, that we had a good deal of freedom on the whole. When my father had gone to his office in the mornings, my mother into town and Kate was occupied about the house, we did as we liked. I don't know what the boys did, but I roamed the district, sometimes alone, sometimes in company with any likely-looking gang that was going about. So long as we appeared punctually at meals few questions were asked, and if I had had the sense to keep quiet I could have done as I liked about my friends. But I hadn't. I had to burst out with my enthusiasms. In the case of Dora Smith this was disastrous.

I fell in with Dora somehow in my wanderings and she entranced me at first sight. She was two years older than I was and much larger. She had bright red hair hanging against her cheeks, which were of a different but equally bright red. She never wore a hat, which was unusual and hardly respectable in those days; her stockings were always coming down and she seemed to be bursting out of her frocks which showed the strain of containing her at every seam and button.

But there was a grand vitality about Dora; her nostrils curved as she sniffed up the breath of life like a lively young horse. She turned her toes out as she walked. I suppose she had flat feet, really; but they gave a noble arrogance to her gait, or so it seemed to me, and I tried to turn out mine in imitation.

The Smiths were not approved of in the neighbourhood. It was said that they owed so much money to the tradespeople that none would serve them any more. They had a spectacular grandfather and had, I think, inherited their reputation from him. This old man had afforded tales for the town for years. After a wild youth, he married and produced a large family which suddenly, or so it seemed, palled upon him. So he turned them in a body out of doors because, he said, he was sick of the sight of them. He then proceeded to live as he chose, which was to get roaring drunk with frequency, and to be at all times extremely rude and outspoken.

Stories of this grandfather formed a great part of Dora Smith's conversation, and the old man assumed legendary proportions in my eyes. I longed to see him for myself, and I became more than ever attached to Dora when she said she would perhaps take me one day to the big dark house where her grandfather now lived quite alone.

'But we shall have to be terribly careful,' she warned. 'Because he might throw a bottle at us if he's in the mood.'

I was thrilled by the dramatic possibilities of the visit and lived in hopes of the worst.

Dora and I had some grand times together before they were put a stop to. We chased about the streets, Dora clutching at her stockings as she ran, her red hair flying, urging me on to goodness knows what. The streets round our house were all quiet and cannot have held much excitement, but we were excited. We made raids of all sorts. We would dash in among the boys going home from the school at the corner, snatch off their caps and throw them over walls and fly off into other people's gardens for safety.

We made completely free of other people's gardens, and one of our games was to work our way right round the garden of some big house, dodging gardeners. We would choose not to be seen at times, but other times Dora would walk nonchalantly across the lawns in full view of the windows.

All might have been well if my admiration of Dora had not grown beyond the bounds of silence. But she told me of such a wildly thrilling exploit at last that I could not keep quiet about it. I unwisely chose to blurt it out one dinner-time when my father was there.

I sat on one side of the table, my two brothers opposite: my father at one end and my mother at the other. All was peace. But as I ate, my breast swelled with pride in Dora and I felt I had to tell them about her.

'Dora Smith is the bravest girl in the world,' I said.

My brothers scoffed, not with words, but with snorts through the nose, at the idea of any girl being brave. But my father was encouraging.

'And who is Dora Smith?' he asked mildly.

'Oh, you know,' said my mother. 'Old Mr Smith of Pennfield.'

'Oh, *that* family,' said my father. 'Well, why is Dora Smith the bravest girl in the world?'

'Well, d'you know what she did?' I said. 'Last night when she went upstairs she found a man on the landing. A tramp it was – all in rags, and she was all alone in the house, and she didn't know what to do, so d'you know what she did? She hit him on the head and she stuffed him down the lavatory with a red-hot poker.'

This dramatic announcement was not received as I expected. There was a loud cackle of laughter from my brothers across the table, but my father did not laugh. It would have been better if he had.

He frowned, and my father's frown is portentous; he has such bushy eyebrows.

'Tchah ... ' he exclaimed with such startling disgust that I gaped in alarm.

'You mustn't play with this girl,' he went on. 'You understand now?'

I couldn't grasp it. I couldn't understand. My brothers were still convulsed across the table. What was there – what could there be in Dora Smith's bravery that made them laugh and my father angry?

'But why can't I play with her?' I faltered.

'Because she's not a fit companion for you. Such vulgar rubbish ....'

A slow shame filled me. I thought I should not have mentioned the lavatory.

In a moment I tried to get this cruel verdict reversed.

'Please let me play with her.'

'No,' said my father sternly. 'You'll have nothing to do with her. A wild, lying, boastful family ... and this girl's evidently like the rest of them. You'll have nothing to do with her. Remember.'

I knew it was hopeless. A lump rose in my throat, powerful cords tugged at the corners of my mouth. I struggled to swallow the lump and to resist the downward pull of the cords. It was terrible to have to cry before other people. I prodded the cold mutton on my plate with my fork, until my mother told me to stop. Not play with Dora! ... It was terrible. There was no one like her. I loved her, and we had such fun. And what would she think? What would she do? I should never see her grandfather now, never do anything exciting again. And all because she had been so brave as to push a tramp down the lavatory with a red-hot poker. I was completely bewildered.

But I dared not disobey my father. I did not go out of the garden for days, in case I should meet Dora. I hung about miserably, wondering what she was doing, what she was thinking. I saw her once or twice, going slowly past the house, tipping up to look through the hedge, looking up at the windows, but she never came to ask for me. She must have known she was not approved of.

Shortly after this the Smiths removed from the neighbourhood, but a year or two later, Dora and I found ourselves at the same school. I was still self-conscious about my abandonment of her, she was older and the circumstances of her life had already had their effect on her. She was harder, or perhaps more sensitive. She realized, I suppose, from my behaviour, that I had been forbidden to play with her, and she took it out of me by scoffing at all I did and said.

One morning we were walking home from school with five or six other girls. There had been a big ball the night before and I was full of the dress my mother had worn. It seemed to me the loveliest dress in the world. It was of duck-egg blue satin with pearl embroideries, and I was busy describing it to the girls.

'It had loops of real pearls hanging down over her shoulders,' I said, and all the little girls were impressed and drew in their breath, when from Dora Smith, walking aloof, stalking with her head in the air, her nostrils curled and her feet turned out, came a shattering remark:

'You are a liar.'

This was awful. We said 'fibber' when we had to say anything of the sort. But she said 'liar' and she said it about me. Taken aback and very shocked, I peered round the string of girls and said:

'I am not. It's perfectly true.'

'Of course it isn't,' said Dora, stalking on. 'You're a liar. If there are any pearls on your mother's dress they are imitation, but I don't suppose there are any pearls on it at all.'

This was too much. With a howl I rushed at her and hit her.

'There are pearls on my mother's dress. It's covered with pearls.'

But Dora wouldn't fight me. She caught my arms and pinned them down and shook me slightly, gazing at me with her strange red-brown eyes.

'You little liar,' she said between her teeth. But her eyes said much more. They said something I could only dimly apprehend. Then she cast me off and stalked quickly up the hill before us.

I came to myself.

'I'll show you the pearls,' I shouted after her. 'I'll bring the dress this afternoon and I'll *show* you them.'

She did not answer. I was left to justify myself to the girls.

'It's covered with pearls,' I insisted. 'Simply covered. They hang all round the neck as well as round the shoulders and there's sort of pearl lace down the front....'

How I managed to get out of the house that afternoon with my mother's ball dress crushed into a paper parcel I don't know, but manage it I did. I marched into form with it under my arm and crammed it into my desk, and after school I undid it and spread it out, sadly creased, to view.

'There!' I said, looking triumphantly at Dora.

She did no more than glance at it contemptuously.

'Do you call these real?' she said, flicking one of the pearl drops with a finger.

'Of course they're real,' I said.

'Of course they're not,' she said. 'You *duffer.*'

My triumph collapsed. I realised she was right. I was a duffer. I had believed the pearls were real. I don't know why; I don't suppose anyone had said they were. I had never imagined they could be anything else. But Dora Smith had shown me to be a simpleton.

She had shown me up not only to the girls but to myself. One could believe too much, it seemed. I had believed her when she said she had stuffed the man down the lavatory with the red-hot

76

poker, and I had believed the pearls on my mother's dress to be real. Somehow one thing after another was turning out not to be *true*.

I should think that about this time I began to be cautious in acceptance.

Starting points

1. *Begin by making one list of all those qualities Dora has that the girl admires her for. Then make another list of those qualities which make her parents disapprove of Dora. Use your lists to help you answer the following questions by talking them over in a small group:*
   - *Is Dora a friend to the girl?*
   - *What qualities do you admire most in a friend?*

2. *Re-read what the opening of the story says about '**the power of grown-up people.**' Discuss what effect this power has in the story. Then talk about a time when you were affected by the power of an adult. It may have been when an adult prevented you from doing something you wished to do or a quite different situation. Compare how you felt with the feelings of the girl in the story.*

3. *Choose either the scene at the dinner-table or the episode of the pearly dress. In a small group, prepare to act out your scene, trying to show accurately how the various characters felt as well as the drama of what happens. Present your version to another group or to the whole class and use their helpful comments for any improvements you have time to make.*

4. *The girl in the story says, '**One could believe too much**'. Note down why you think she says this, then compare your notes with another person. Still with your partner, talk about a time when you believed in something that turned out to be untrue. Use your experience (and any suggestions your partner makes) as the basis for a story of your own.*

FOOTBALL CRAZY

Arthur Barton

SPORTS Days at my elementary school were held on the tip – one of the small pieces of spare ground scattered about the town. They were repositories for tins, old mattresses, prams and bedsteads, dumps for the sweeps' soot, free storage space for timber baulks and iron pipes belonging to the North Eastern Railway. Near the middle there was always a hard fairly clear area where football was played for nine months of the year and cricket tolerated for three. On such a tip some summer afternoon our school would hold its annual sports day.

There was no need to mark out the 'field'. Mr Harris would take Standard 7 and spend a pleasant morning clearing away the larger stones, and fixing the only two essential points – a start and a winning post.

When school assembled for the afternoon we took off our jackets or jerseys, tucked frocks into knickers (our girls' school joined us on rare occasions like Sports Day), laced our boots tightly, and were ready. Miss Grey's portable gramophone was brought out and placed on a little table in the yard, and to the miniature roar of a Guards band playing 'With Sword and Lance' we marched our fifty yards to the tip which was just behind the drill-hall opposite the school.

Here Mr Macdonald, the headmaster, sat at a trestle table with a huge sheet of paper pinned to a drawing board in front of him. He recorded the winners. Near him on another table were the prizes, guarded by Miss Dean. One would have supposed her forty years of vigilance sufficient, but she was reinforced by a tall policeman.

This was because of our spectators. Except for a knot of vociferously partisan mothers they were all men. Half our fathers and brothers were already workless in the post-war slump and they formed the bulk of the crowd.

Young Mr Jenkins was the judge and judging was a job that needed a sharp eye and great firmness. To spot the first three from among the dozen figures that flailed their way down the tip and converged upon poor Mr Jenkins in a sweaty determined mob took some doing.

I noticed at first that he was grateful to a quiet workman squatting on his hunkers near the winning post who helped him to pick the winners. But in the interval, while the whole school crowded round the Italian's pony cart for ice-cream cornets, I heard Miss Grey tell him that the last four winners were all this man's children. After the interval Mr MacDonald did the judging himself.

At last it was over; even the staff race which was Mr MacDonald's annual and ill-advised concession to democracy. Mr Jenkins retrieved a little of his lost prestige by winning it, but, after all, he was barely twenty and he did try to give the race to Miss Grey, but she tripped over a half-buried chimney pot and was supported from the stricken field.

While the distant gramophone played 'Liebestraume', the vicar of Christ Church distributed the prizes: pocket books, pencils, combs, knives and jewellery that Miss Dean had bought at Piper's Penny Bazaar during the dinner hour.

'Many run,' he murmured ruefully, 'but one receiveth the prize.' His mild Oxford voice effaced for a moment our grimy montage of cranes and condensers.

I noticed Lily Wilson, one of the fleetest girls, being congratulated by her father. She caught my eye and smiled in affected pleasure. 'Me da's delighted with us, Barty. He won thirty bob from his mates, and he's given us ten to get a pair of dance shoes. I think I'll get silver.'

As we dispersed, Lily, who lived in Grenville Street not far from me, and was still flushed with victory, brought me over a big cornet.

Sports Day, like all annual events, was soon forgotten. Cricket survived in a desultory way through the summer holiday but with the coming of September football resumed its paramount importance. How could it be otherwise when we lived midway between Newcastle and Sunderland in the great days of wee Hughie Gallagher and Dave Halliday?

We were all football crazy in Grenville Street. They were in Raleigh Street and Drake Court and Hawkins Avenue, too. You'd have expected us to be sea-minded when our streets had names like that, but the sea was three whole miles away, and we seldom got so far, though the east wind sometimes had salt in it and you could hear Souter Point foghorn often on winter evenings.

Even then we played football in the tiny circle of radiance round our lamp, sending young Ronnie out into damp invisibility every few minutes to find the lost ball, while we danced on and off the pavement to keep warm and grimaced at our enormous shadows.

But football wasn't much fun unless you had a real ball like the one we had at school. Raleigh Street had one, but they were a step higher socially than we were – trimmers and platers lived there – big money men – even one or two clerks who wore bowlers and went to work 'dressed'. Our fathers were overalled to a man; crane-drivers, riveters and labourers, and our pocket money was hardly ever more than the statutory penny. If we had pooled our resources it would have taken the whole season to buy the bladder, never mind the case.

Rinso Selby called us all together one dry frosty evening, and we sat round the lamp like a pack of jersey-clad nondescript wolves while he told us how the miracle of ball-owning Raleigh Street might be repeated here in humbler Grenville. Rinso was our leader, a tall boy of nearly fourteen. He played for the school team. 'There's only one way I can see us getting a ball,' he said, 'and that's to have a bazaar.'

We cheered him to the echo. Bazaars were great. First you got someone to lend you their backyard to have it in, and then you collected things to sell. The girls were always doing it in summer, with cold custard doing duty for ice-cream, and red jelly, and scent cards, and lavender bags, and such like rubbish.

No one had ever had one in winter before, but Rinso thought it would be just as easy if we all put our backs into it. The lamplight glinted on his Scout badge and outlined his resolute chin, and we felt momentarily capable of anything.

First we had to find a backyard. 'Lily Wilson's!' shouted Sam.

Lily had left school soon after Sports Day, and her red hair was now piled on top of her head in a grown-up bun.

She kept house for her widowed father who drank and was usually amiable, not caring what she did as long as his pot-pie was ready when he came in from the blast furnaces where he had been lucky enough to find a temporary job.

Some nostalgia for school had made her keep one of her own in

80

her backyard all the summer holiday, and Ritchie Caldwell claimed that she'd done more to teach him to read than Miss Madison and her cane in a whole year in Standard 2.

'You may have it with pleasure next Saturday,' said Lily in her schoolteacher voice that we were all rather afraid of – then, spoiling it a bit, 'Me da'll be in the Golden Fleece till chucking-out time.' Lily's backyard contained an old rain-sodden table from which we could sell things, and a pile of orange boxes waiting to be chopped up for firewood. Rinso's eyes lit up.

'Does yer want them boxes, Lily?'

She tossed her head in affectionate contempt.

'He'll never notice they're gone the way he'll be when he comes in, hinneys,' she said.

Rinso's idea was to light a fire in the corner of the yard and cook sausages over it in an army dixie. Then we'd beg a stale loaf or two at Grannie Grieves's bakery and make hot dogs. Ronnie and I were deputed to do this. Of course we had no sausages, but everyone bought an occasional length of 'butcher's sausage', as we called the long coil that lay piled on an enormous plate on every counter, and throughout the week we all snapped a few inches off and smuggled them in our none-too-clean handkerchiefs to Lily, who stored them in a basin under the mangle and covered it with a tin plate to keep the cats off.

What to sell presented the next problem. We weren't girls and couldn't cook jam tarts and things like that. We collected vast piles of comics and everyone brought a toy he'd got tired of. Sam's mother made us a bedroom jug of lemonade from a packet of crystals, and we used clean one-pound jam-jars to drink from. Fred wrote hundreds of lines for the few grammar-school types who might come and were always glad of reserves for future impositions. He chose 'Bells of Shandon' because its lines were the shortest in the book. I helped him and together we chanted:

'Whose sounds so wild would,
In days of childhood,
Fling round my cradle,
Their magic spells',

as we knocked them off at twopence a hundred.

Winnie and Gladys made us a couple of trays of pink nutty toffee. And Lily offered all she had – herself. It was arranged that she would sell kisses to all comers at a penny each, and a roaring trade was expected. Lily's kisses were popular and famous. That

81

was how she rewarded us when we played schools for getting our sums right. Unfortunately, being no good at arithmetic I had never qualified, but by the Saturday of the bazaar I had amassed fourpence by fetching coal from the local depot in an iron-shod wheelbarrow to four old couples who had no children to send. We all bought our coal that way – a hundred-weight at a time – except the rich across the park. They sometimes bought a ton at once – it cost a whole pound. I had never kissed any of the girls except Winnie, who tasted of gob-stoppers and was inclined to dribble, so I was rather looking forward to Lily's which were said to be as long and expert as Velma Banky's in a Valentino film.

The day of the bazaar was bright and clear, much to our satisfaction. It was bitterly cold, but the ice soon melted on the pools between the cobbles. We got our 'messages' over as soon as possible – then to Wilson's yard to set out our bazaar. Ronnie and I lighted our fire Scout fashion and put our sections of sausage into the dixie. The table was piled high with comics and tarnished toys and toffee. On the back door Lily had chalked 'Grand Football Bazaar. Opening at 2 p.m.', and Rinso had put notices in four or five of the little house-shops we had at every street corner. In any case, the news had spread to all the neighbouring streets and round school and by half past one a pushing mob was filling the back lane and yelling for admission. The smell of frying sausage wafted out to their eager noses. Ronnie sliced the stale bread with some difficulty. His Scout knife was a bit blunt after chopping up the orange boxes.

Lily, in a pink blouse, took up her stance by the lavatory door. This was the only place where the kisses could be exchanged in privacy and a suitable semi-darkness.

Rinso stood at the table mounting guard over an empty bait-can which we hoped to fill with the accumulated pocket money of a dozen streets in the next hour. He nodded to Fred and the door was unbolted. Like a barbarian horde the customers surged in – and made straight for Lily.

An hour later it was all over, and we were sitting round the red ashes of our cooking fire, dipping pieces of stale bread into the still sizzling dregs of sausage fat. The lemonade jug was empty. Abandoned jam-jars littered the yard. Not a comic, not a toy, not a lump of toffee was left. Lily, dishevelled but triumphant, sat enthroned on the inverted rain-barrel, a Woodbine glowing between her somewhat overworked lips.

Rinso tipped the heavy bait-tin on to the table-top and we counted the takings, huddled over them like a rugger scrum. It looked a lot, but there was only ten and sevenpence, three French pennies, a token that said 'Long live Victoria', and an Indian coin of doubtful value.

Would this buy a ball, a real case ball, splendid and brown and leather-smelling, with a lace to tighten and beautiful stitched panels?

Rinso shook his head sadly. We were five shillings short – a lot of money then.

'Can't ye buy a bladder,' suggested Winnie, 'and get the case later?' Rinso shook his head again. We'd done this before and the bladder had lasted only three days. It could not survive our vigorous bootings.

'We must get this last five bob,' said Rinso as if it were a trivial sum. All eyes turned to Lily, but sixty more favours were rather a lot to ask, and in any case where could customers be found at this late hour when pocket money had all been spent?

I still had my fourpence, but this didn't seem the time to press Lily in any sense, so I slipped it regretfully into the can.

Grimly, hands thrust in pockets, we slouched up the street looking rather hopelessly for lost coins that eager customers might have dropped in the gutter.

Lily drew Winnie aside and they ran off back to Lily's house. The rest of us hung about in the bitter east wind dribbling a stone round one another, full of disappointment.

'So near and yet so far,' muttered Ronnie, as Rinso jingled the takings in his pockets.

A door slammed down the street and Lily and Winnie were running back towards us. Lily carried a brown-paper parcel. 'Howway,' she said, 'I've had an inspiration.'

We followed her down into town to an alley near the school clinic where the shop was that we were all looking for. Its three dirty brass balls glinted in the dusk. In the window were watches and rings and china jugs, and worn navy suits, and pictures of Highland cattle – all the sad debris of improvident homes.

We looked at them while the girls were inside. In a few minutes they came out again, Lily pale but triumphant.

'We're all right, lads,' she said, 'he's give us five bob on them.'

'What on, Lily?' I asked seeing she was upset.

'Me silver dancing shoes,' she replied, turning away to hide her tears. 'I've only worn them once to the Mechanics' Dance.'

'We'll get them back for you, Lily,' promised Rinso, as we hurried round to the leather shop, but we knew, and so did she, that we never would.

What made her do it? Love, I suppose. Love for Rinso, who hadn't even kissed her that afternoon and probably never would. His eyes were only for the ball, which he bounced all the way home, and his mind on the team he would be able to train, and how we would beat Raleigh Street at last and with our own ball on some not too distant Saturday.

And we did. I even remember the score, 4–2. This isn't because I scored a goal. I've never done that in my life, but because it was the day Lily got her dancing shoes back.

Somehow I was the only one in the street that afternoon when she came running up.

'Guess what, Barty!' she said excitingly. 'Me da's three-horse roller's come up and he's give us five bob.'

I remembered Sports Day far back in the summer when her own fleetness had won her the original price of her beloved shoes.

Together we went down the street to the pawnshop, past the Mechanics' where a poster said 'Select Dance Tonight', and Lily took in her preciously preserved ticket and came out with them under her arm.

On our way back, as the first gas lamps flickered into life and threw their wan pools of radiance on the already frosty pavements, she took my arm suddenly and steered me into a narrow lane between the Co-op dairy and a chemist's. The boys had been right about Lily's kisses. They were nothing at all like poor Winnie's. It was like drowning in the nicest possible way.

And when we emerged into the teatime street, and she took my hand in hers and we ran together over the railway bridge and back to our street where the ball was being punted about between lamps by Rinso and Ronnie and the rest, I was more than football crazy.

Starting points

1. Talk about sports day at your present school or at one you have recently left. How different is the occasion at Barty's school? Look again at details of the sports day scene in the story and write a report of it for the school magazine at that time.

2. Make notes about a time when you worked very hard to achieve or obtain something that you wanted very much. Mention the reasons you wanted it, your preparations, what happened and what your feelings were. Then, using your notes and working with a partner, listen to each other's stories and compare them with what the Grenville Street children did.

3. Talk about Lily and decide what kind of person she is and why she did the things she did. Re-write the events of the story from her point of view, beginning where she agrees to have the bazaar in her backyard.

4. In a small group, talk about a time when you lost or gave away a treasured possession or when something you valued was broken or taken away from you. How did your behaviour and feelings then compare with Lily's?

ADOLF

D.H. Lawrence

WHEN we were children our father often worked on the night-shift. Once it was spring-time, and he used to arrive home, black and tired, just as we were downstairs in our nightdresses. Then night met morning face to face, and the contact was not always happy. Perhaps it was painful to my father to see us gaily entering upon the day into which he dragged himself soiled and weary. He didn't like going to bed in the spring morning sunshine.

But sometimes he was happy, because of his long walk through the dewy fields in the first daybreak. He loved the open morning, the crystal and the space, after a night down pit. He watched every bird, every stir in the trembling grass, answered the whinnying of the peewits and tweeted to the wrens. If he could, he also would have whinnied and tweeted and whistled in a native language that wasn't human. He liked non-human things best.

One sunny morning we were all sitting at table when we heard his heavy slurring walk up the entry. We became uneasy. His was always a disturbing presence, trammelling. He passed the window darkly, and we heard him go into the scullery and put down his tin bottle. But directly he came into the kitchen we felt at once that he had something to communicate. No one spoke. We watched his black face for a second.

'Give me a drink,' he said.

My mother hastily poured out his tea. He went to pour it out into his saucer. But instead of drinking it he suddenly put something on the table among the tea-cups. A tiny brown rabbit! A small rabbit, a mere morsel, sitting against the bread as still as if it were a made thing.

'A rabbit! a young one! Who gave it to you, Father?'

But he laughed, enigmatically, with a sliding motion of his yellow-gray eyes, and went to take off his coat. We pounced on the rabbit.

'Is it alive? Can you feel its heart beat?'

My father came back and sat down heavily in his armchair. He dragged his saucer to him, and blew his tea, pushing out his red lips under his black moustache.

'Where did you get it, Father?'

'I picked it up,' he said, wiping his fore-arm over his mouth and beard.

'Where?'

'It's a wild one!' came my mother's quick voice.

'Yes, it is.'

'Then why did you bring it?' cried my mother.

'Oh, we wanted it,' came our cry.

'Yes, I've no doubt you did,' retorted my mother. But she was drowned in our clamour of questions. On the field-path my father had found a dead mother rabbit and three dead little ones – this one alive, but unmoving.

'But what had killed them, Daddy?'

'I couldn't say, my child. I s'd think she'd aten something.'

'Why did you bring it!' again my mother's voice of condemnation. 'You know what it will be.'

My father made no answer, but we were loud in protest.

'He must bring it. It's not big enough to live by itself.'

'It would die,' we shouted.

'Yes, and it will die now. And then there'll be another outcry.'

My mother set her face against the tragedy of dead pets. Our hearts sank.

'It won't die, Father, will it? Why will it? It won't.'

'I s'd think not,' said my father.

'You know well enough it will. Haven't we had it all before!' said my mother.

'They dunna always pine,' replied my father testily.

But my mother reminded him of other little wild animals he had brought, which had sulked and refused to live, and brought storms of tears and trouble in our house of lunatics. Trouble fell on us. The little rabbit sat on our lap, unmoving, its eyes wide and dark. We brought it milk, warm milk, and held it to its nose. It sat as still as if it was far away, retreated down some deep burrow, hidden, oblivious. We wetted its mouth and whiskers with drops of milk.

It gave no sign, did not even shake off the wet, white drops. Somebody began to shed a few secret tears.

'What did I say?' cried my mother. 'Take it and put it down in the field.'

Her command was in vain. We were driven to get dressed for school. There sat the rabbit. It was like a tiny obscure cloud. Watching it, the emotions died out of the breast. Useless to love it, to yearn over it. Its little feelings were all ambushed. They must be circumvented. Love and affection were a trespass upon it. A little wild thing, it became more mute and asphyxiated still in its own arrest, when we approached with love. We must not love it. We must circumvent it, for its own existence.

So I passed the order to my sister and mother. The rabbit was not to be spoken to, or even looked at. Wrapping it in a piece of flannel, I put it in an obscure corner of the cold parlour, and put a saucer of milk before its nose. My mother was forbidden to enter the parlour while we were at school.

'As if I should take any notice of your nonsense,' she cried, affronted. Yet I doubt if she ventured into the parlour.

At midday, after school, creeping into the front room, there we saw the rabbit still and unmoving in the piece of flannel. Strange grey-brown neutralisation of life, still living! It was a sore problem to us.

'Why won't it drink its milk, Mother?' we whispered. Our father was asleep.

'It prefers to sulk its life away, silly little thing.'

A profound problem. Prefers to sulk its life away!
We put young dandelion leaves to its nose. The sphinx was not more oblivious. Yet its eye was bright.

At teatime, however, it had hopped a few inches, out of its flannel, and there it sat again, uncovered, a little solid cloud of muteness, with unmoving whiskers. Only its side palpitated slightly with life.

Darkness came. My father set out for work. The rabbit was still unmoving. Dumb despair was coming over the sisters, a threat of tears before bedtime. Clouds of my mother's anger gathered as she muttered against my father's wantonness.

Once more the rabbit was wrapped in the old pit-singlet. But now it was carried into the scullery and put under the copper fireplace, that it might imagine itself inside a burrow. The saucers were placed about, four or five, here and there on the floor, so that if the little creature should chance to hop abroad, it could not fail to come upon some food. After this my mother was allowed to take from the scullery what she wanted and then she was forbidden to open the door.

When morning came and it was light, I went downstairs. Opening the scullery door, I heard a slight scuffle. Then I saw dabbles of milk all over the floor and tiny rabbit-droppings in the saucers. And there was the miscreant, the tips of his ears showing behind a pair of boots. I peeped at him. He sat bright-eyed and askance, twitching his nose and looking at me while not looking at me.

He was alive – very much alive. But we were still afraid to trespass much on his confidence.

'Father!' My father was arrested at the door. 'Father, the rabbit's alive!'

'Back your life it is,' said my father.

'Mind how you go in.'

By evening, however, the little creature was tame, quite tame. He was christened Adolf. We were enchanted by him. We couldn't really love him, because he was wild and loveless to the end. But he was an unmixed delight.

We decided he was too small to live in a hutch – he must live at large in the house. My mother protested, but in vain. He was so tiny. So we had him upstairs, and he dropped tiny pills on the bed and we were enchanted.

Adolf made himself instantly at home. He had the run of the house and was perfectly happy, with his tunnels and his holes behind the furniture.

We loved him to take meals with us. He would sit on the table humping his back, sipping his milk, shaking his whiskers and his tender ears, hopping off and hobbling back to his saucer, with an air of supreme unconcern. Suddenly he was alert. He hobbled a few tiny paces, and reared himself up inquisitively at the sugar-basin. He fluttered his tiny forepaws, and then reached and laid them on the edge of the basin, whilst he craned his thin neck and peeped in. He trembled his whiskers at the sugar, then did his best to lift down a lump.

'*Do* you think I will have it! Animals in the sugar-pot!' cried my mother with a rap of her hand on the table.

Which so delighted the electric Adolf that he flung his hind-quarters and knocked over a cup.

'It's your own fault, Mother. If you left him alone – '

He continued to take tea with us. He rather liked warm tea. And he loved sugar. Having nibbled a lump, he would turn to the butter. There he was shoo'd off by our parent. He soon learned to treat her shooing with indifference. Still, she hated him to put his nose in the food. And he loved to do it. And one day between them they overturned the cream-jug. Adolf deluged his little chest, bounced back in terror, was seized by his little ears by my mother and bounced down on the hearth-rug. There he shivered in momentary discomfort, and suddenly set off in a wild flight to the parlour.

This last was his happy hunting-ground. He had cultivated the bad habit of pensively nibbling certain bits of cloth in the hearth-rug. When chased from this pasture, he would retreat under the sofa. There he would twinkle in meditation until suddenly, no one knew why, he would go off like an alarm clock. With a sudden bumping scuffle he would whirl out of the room, going through the doorway with his little ears flying. Then we would hear his thunderbolt hurtling in the parlour, but before we could follow, the wild streak of Adolf would flash past us, on an electric wind that swept him round the scullery and carried him back, a little mad thing, flying possessed like a ball round the parlour. After which ebullition he would sit in a corner composed and distant, twitching his whiskers in abstract meditation. And it was in vain we questioned him about his outbursts. He just went off like a gun, and was as calm after it as a gun that smokes placidly.

Alas! he grew up rapidly. It was almost impossible to keep him from the outer door.

One day, as we were playing by the stile, I saw his brown shadow loiter across the road and pass into the field that faced the houses. Instantly a cry of 'Adolf!' – a cry he knew full well. And instantly a wind swept him away down the sloping meadow, tail twinkling and zig-zagging through the grass. After him we pelted. It was a strange sight to see him, ears back, his little loins so powerful, flinging the world behind him. We ran ourselves out of breath, but we could not catch him. Then somebody headed him off, and he sat with sudden unconcern, twitching his nose under a bunch of nettles.

His wanderings cost him a shock. One Sunday morning my father had just been quarrelling with a pedlar, and we were

90

hearing the aftermath indoors, when there came a sudden unearthly scream from the yard. We flew out; there sat Adolf cowering under a bench, whilst a great black-and-white cat glowered intently at him a few yards away. Sight not to be forgotten. Adolf rolling back his eyes and parting his strange muzzle in another scream, the cat stretching forward in slow elongation.

Ha! how we hated that cat! How we pursued him over the chapel wall and across the neighbours' gardens. Adolf was still only half-grown.

'Cats!' said my mother. 'Hideous detestable animals! Why do people harbour them?'

But Adolf was becoming too much for her. Suddenly to hear him clumping downstairs when she was alone in the house was startling. And to keep him from the door impossible. Cats prowled outside. It was worse than having a child to look after. Yet we would not have him shut up. He became more lusty, more callous than ever. He was a strong kicker, and many a scratch on face and arms did we owe to him. But he brought his own doom on himself. The lace curtains in the parlour – my mother was rather proud of them – fell on the floor very full. One of Adolf's joys was to scuffle wildly through them as though through some foamy undergrowth. He had already torn rents in them.

One day he entangled himself altogether. He kicked, he whirled round in a mad nebulous inferno. He screamed – and brought down the curtain-rod with a smash, right on the best beloved geranium just as my mother rushed in. She extricated him, but she never forgave him.

Even we understood that he must go. It was decided, after a long deliberation, that my father should carry him back to the wild woods. Once again he was stowed into the great pocket of the pit-jacket.

'Best pop him i' the pot,' said my father, who enjoyed raising the wind of indignation.

And so, next day, our father said that Adolf, set down on the edge of the coppice, had hopped away with utmost indifference, neither elated nor moved. We heard it and believed. But many, many were the heart-searchings. How would the other rabbits receive him? Would they smell his tameness, his humanised degradation, and rend him? My mother pooh-poohed the extravagant idea.

However, he was gone, and we were rather relieved. My father kept an eye open for him. He declared that several times passing the coppice in the early morning, he had seen Adolf peeping through the nettle-stalks. He had called him in an odd, high-voiced, cajoling fashion. But Adolf had not responded. Wildness gains so soon upon its creatures. And they become so contemptuous then of our tame presence. So it seemed to me. I myself would go to the edge of the coppice, and call softly. I myself would imagine bright eyes between the nettle-stalks, flash of a white scornful tail past the bracken. That insolent white tail, as Adolf turned his flank on us.

Starting points

1. *Imagine that you are one of the children in the story and that you have been asked to give a talk about a pet to your class at school. Using details from the story, make notes and a plan for your talk about Adolf. Make the talk as vivid and entertaining as you can. Try the talk on your own class or in your own group.*

2. *Look through the story again and jot down how the mother feels about Adolf (and the rest of her family!) at various points in the story. Then use these notes to talk in your group about what kind of person she is. Finally, re-tell the story from her point of view, beginning where Adolf began to take meals with the family and ending where the geranium is crushed.*

3. *Make a list of all the wild things that Adolf does in the story and those descriptions of his attitude and behaviour that particularly show his wildness. Then, in your group, talk about why the father 'liked* **non-human things best***'. How far do you agree with him?*

4. *Talk in your group about any wild animal or bird that you kept for a time or one that visited your house or garden. Then write your story of the creature in such a way as to show your own feelings about it as well as its feelings towards you.*